FOR LUST

(A Morgan Cross FBI Suspense Thriller—Book Three)

BLAKE PIERCE

Blake Pierce

Blake Pierce is the USA Today bestselling author of the RILEY PAGE mystery series, which includes seventeen books. Blake Pierce is also the author of the MACKENZIE WHITE mystery series, comprising fourteen books; of the AVERY BLACK mystery series, comprising six books; of the KERI LOCKE mystery series, comprising five books; of the MAKING OF RILEY PAIGE mystery series, comprising six books; of the KATE WISE mystery series, comprising seven books; of the CHLOE FINE psychological suspense mystery, comprising six books; of the JESSIE HUNT psychological suspense thriller series, comprising twenty-eight books; of the AU PAIR psychological suspense thriller series, comprising three books; of the ZOE PRIME mystery series, comprising six books; of the ADELE SHARP mystery series, comprising sixteen books, of the EUROPEAN VOYAGE cozy mystery series, comprising six books; of the LAURA FROST FBI suspense thriller, comprising eleven books; of the ELLA DARK FBI suspense thriller, comprising sixteen books (and counting); of the A YEAR IN EUROPE cozy mystery series, comprising nine books, of the AVA GOLD mystery series, comprising six books; of the RACHEL GIFT mystery series, comprising ten books (and counting); of the VALERIE LAW mystery series, comprising nine books (and counting); of the PAIGE KING mystery series, comprising eight books (and counting); of the MAY MOORE mystery series, comprising eleven books; of the CORA SHIELDS mystery series, comprising eight books (and counting); of the NICKY LYONS mystery series, comprising eight books (and counting), of the CAMI LARK mystery series, comprising eight books (and counting), of the AMBER YOUNG mystery series, comprising five books (and counting), of the DAISY FORTUNE mystery series, comprising five books (and counting), of the FIONA RED mystery series, comprising eight books (and counting), of the FAITH BOLD mystery series, comprising eight books (and counting), of the JULIETTE HART mystery series, comprising five books (and counting), of the MORGAN CROSS mystery series, comprising five books (and counting), and of the new FINN WRIGHT mystery series, comprising five books (and counting).

An avid reader and lifelong fan of the mystery and thriller genres, Blake loves to hear from you, so please feel free to visit www.blakepierceauthor.com to learn more and stay in touch.

ISBN: 978-1-0943-8250-0

BOOKS BY BLAKE PIERCE

FINN WRIGHT MYSTERY SERIES
WHEN YOU'RE MINE (Book #1)
WHEN YOU'RE SAFE (Book #2)
WHEN YOU'RE CLOSE (Book #3)
WHEN YOU'RE SLEEPING (Book #4)
WHEN YOU'RE SANE (Book #5)

MORGAN CROSS MYSTERY SERIES
FOR YOU (Book #1)
FOR RAGE (Book #2)
FOR LUST (Book #3)
FOR WRATH (Book #4)
FOREVER (Book #5)

JULIETTE HART MYSTERY SERIES
NOTHING TO FEAR (Book #1)
NOTHING THERE (Book #2)
NOTHING WATCHING (Book #3)
NOTHING HIDING (Book #4)
NOTHING LEFT (Book #5)

FAITH BOLD MYSTERY SERIES
SO LONG (Book #1)
SO COLD (Book #2)
SO SCARED (Book #3)
SO NORMAL (Book #4)
SO FAR GONE (Book #5)
SO LOST (Book #6)
SO ALONE (Book #7)
SO FORGOTTEN (Book #8)

FIONA RED MYSTERY SERIES
LET HER GO (Book #1)
LET HER BE (Book #2)
LET HER HOPE (Book #3)

LET HER WISH (Book #4)
LET HER LIVE (Book #5)
LET HER RUN (Book #6)
LET HER HIDE (Book #7)
LET HER BELIEVE (Book #8)

DAISY FORTUNE MYSTERY SERIES
NEED YOU (Book #1)
CLAIM YOU (Book #2)
CRAVE YOU (Book #3)
CHOOSE YOU (Book #4)
CHASE YOU (Book #5)

AMBER YOUNG MYSTERY SERIES
ABSENT PITY (Book #1)
ABSENT REMORSE (Book #2)
ABSENT FEELING (Book #3)
ABSENT MERCY (Book #4)
ABSENT REASON (Book #5)

CAMI LARK MYSTERY SERIES
JUST ME (Book #1)
JUST OUTSIDE (Book #2)
JUST RIGHT (Book #3)
JUST FORGET (Book #4)
JUST ONCE (Book #5)
JUST HIDE (Book #6)
JUST NOW (Book #7)
JUST HOPE (Book #8)

NICKY LYONS MYSTERY SERIES
ALL MINE (Book #1)
ALL HIS (Book #2)
ALL HE SEES (Book #3)
ALL ALONE (Book #4)
ALL FOR ONE (Book #5)
ALL HE TAKES (Book #6)
ALL FOR ME (Book #7)
ALL IN (Book #8)

CORA SHIELDS MYSTERY SERIES
UNDONE (Book #1)
UNWANTED (Book #2)
UNHINGED (Book #3)
UNSAID (Book #4)
UNGLUED (Book #5)
UNSTABLE (Book #6)
UNKNOWN (Book #7)
UNAWARE (Book #8)

MAY MOORE SUSPENSE THRILLER
NEVER RUN (Book #1)
NEVER TELL (Book #2)
NEVER LIVE (Book #3)
NEVER HIDE (Book #4)
NEVER FORGIVE (Book #5)
NEVER AGAIN (Book #6)
NEVER LOOK BACK (Book #7)
NEVER FORGET (Book #8)
NEVER LET GO (Book #9)
NEVER PRETEND (Book #10)
NEVER HESITATE (Book #11)

PAIGE KING MYSTERY SERIES
THE GIRL HE PINED (Book #1)
THE GIRL HE CHOSE (Book #2)
THE GIRL HE TOOK (Book #3)
THE GIRL HE WISHED (Book #4)
THE GIRL HE CROWNED (Book #5)
THE GIRL HE WATCHED (Book #6)
THE GIRL HE WANTED (Book #7)
THE GIRL HE CLAIMED (Book #8)

VALERIE LAW MYSTERY SERIES
NO MERCY (Book #1)
NO PITY (Book #2)
NO FEAR (Book #3)
NO SLEEP (Book #4)
NO QUARTER (Book #5)
NO CHANCE (Book #6)

NO REFUGE (Book #7)
NO GRACE (Book #8)
NO ESCAPE (Book #9)

RACHEL GIFT MYSTERY SERIES
HER LAST WISH (Book #1)
HER LAST CHANCE (Book #2)
HER LAST HOPE (Book #3)
HER LAST FEAR (Book #4)
HER LAST CHOICE (Book #5)
HER LAST BREATH (Book #6)
HER LAST MISTAKE (Book #7)
HER LAST DESIRE (Book #8)
HER LAST REGRET (Book #9)
HER LAST HOUR (Book #10)

AVA GOLD MYSTERY SERIES
CITY OF PREY (Book #1)
CITY OF FEAR (Book #2)
CITY OF BONES (Book #3)
CITY OF GHOSTS (Book #4)
CITY OF DEATH (Book #5)
CITY OF VICE (Book #6)

A YEAR IN EUROPE
A MURDER IN PARIS (Book #1)
DEATH IN FLORENCE (Book #2)
VENGEANCE IN VIENNA (Book #3)
A FATALITY IN SPAIN (Book #4)

ELLA DARK FBI SUSPENSE THRILLER
GIRL, ALONE (Book #1)
GIRL, TAKEN (Book #2)
GIRL, HUNTED (Book #3)
GIRL, SILENCED (Book #4)
GIRL, VANISHED (Book 5)
GIRL ERASED (Book #6)
GIRL, FORSAKEN (Book #7)
GIRL, TRAPPED (Book #8)
GIRL, EXPENDABLE (Book #9)

GIRL, ESCAPED (Book #10)
GIRL, HIS (Book #11)
GIRL, LURED (Book #12)
GIRL, MISSING (Book #13)
GIRL, UNKNOWN (Book #14)
GIRL, DECEIVED (Book #15)
GIRL, FORLORN (Book #16)

LAURA FROST FBI SUSPENSE THRILLER
ALREADY GONE (Book #1)
ALREADY SEEN (Book #2)
ALREADY TRAPPED (Book #3)
ALREADY MISSING (Book #4)
ALREADY DEAD (Book #5)
ALREADY TAKEN (Book #6)
ALREADY CHOSEN (Book #7)
ALREADY LOST (Book #8)
ALREADY HIS (Book #9)
ALREADY LURED (Book #10)
ALREADY COLD (Book #11)

EUROPEAN VOYAGE COZY MYSTERY SERIES
MURDER (AND BAKLAVA) (Book #1)
DEATH (AND APPLE STRUDEL) (Book #2)
CRIME (AND LAGER) (Book #3)
MISFORTUNE (AND GOUDA) (Book #4)
CALAMITY (AND A DANISH) (Book #5)
MAYHEM (AND HERRING) (Book #6)

ADELE SHARP MYSTERY SERIES
LEFT TO DIE (Book #1)
LEFT TO RUN (Book #2)
LEFT TO HIDE (Book #3)
LEFT TO KILL (Book #4)
LEFT TO MURDER (Book #5)
LEFT TO ENVY (Book #6)
LEFT TO LAPSE (Book #7)
LEFT TO VANISH (Book #8)
LEFT TO HUNT (Book #9)
LEFT TO FEAR (Book #10)

LEFT TO PREY (Book #11)
LEFT TO LURE (Book #12)
LEFT TO CRAVE (Book #13)
LEFT TO LOATHE (Book #14)
LEFT TO HARM (Book #15)
LEFT TO RUIN (Book #16)

THE AU PAIR SERIES
ALMOST GONE (Book#1)
ALMOST LOST (Book #2)
ALMOST DEAD (Book #3)

ZOE PRIME MYSTERY SERIES
FACE OF DEATH (Book#1)
FACE OF MURDER (Book #2)
FACE OF FEAR (Book #3)
FACE OF MADNESS (Book #4)
FACE OF FURY (Book #5)
FACE OF DARKNESS (Book #6)

A JESSIE HUNT PSYCHOLOGICAL SUSPENSE SERIES
THE PERFECT WIFE (Book #1)
THE PERFECT BLOCK (Book #2)
THE PERFECT HOUSE (Book #3)
THE PERFECT SMILE (Book #4)
THE PERFECT LIE (Book #5)
THE PERFECT LOOK (Book #6)
THE PERFECT AFFAIR (Book #7)
THE PERFECT ALIBI (Book #8)
THE PERFECT NEIGHBOR (Book #9)
THE PERFECT DISGUISE (Book #10)
THE PERFECT SECRET (Book #11)
THE PERFECT FAÇADE (Book #12)
THE PERFECT IMPRESSION (Book #13)
THE PERFECT DECEIT (Book #14)
THE PERFECT MISTRESS (Book #15)
THE PERFECT IMAGE (Book #16)
THE PERFECT VEIL (Book #17)
THE PERFECT INDISCRETION (Book #18)
THE PERFECT RUMOR (Book #19)

THE PERFECT COUPLE (Book #20)
THE PERFECT MURDER (Book #21)
THE PERFECT HUSBAND (Book #22)
THE PERFECT SCANDAL (Book #23)
THE PERFECT MASK (Book #24)
THE PERFECT RUSE (Book #25)
THE PERFECT VENEER (Book #26)
THE PERFECT PEOPLE (Book #27)
THE PERFECT WITNESS (Book #28)

CHLOE FINE PSYCHOLOGICAL SUSPENSE SERIES
NEXT DOOR (Book #1)
A NEIGHBOR'S LIE (Book #2)
CUL DE SAC (Book #3)
SILENT NEIGHBOR (Book #4)
HOMECOMING (Book #5)
TINTED WINDOWS (Book #6)

KATE WISE MYSTERY SERIES
IF SHE KNEW (Book #1)
IF SHE SAW (Book #2)
IF SHE RAN (Book #3)
IF SHE HID (Book #4)
IF SHE FLED (Book #5)
IF SHE FEARED (Book #6)
IF SHE HEARD (Book #7)

THE MAKING OF RILEY PAIGE SERIES
WATCHING (Book #1)
WAITING (Book #2)
LURING (Book #3)
TAKING (Book #4)
STALKING (Book #5)
KILLING (Book #6)

RILEY PAIGE MYSTERY SERIES
ONCE GONE (Book #1)
ONCE TAKEN (Book #2)
ONCE CRAVED (Book #3)
ONCE LURED (Book #4)

ONCE HUNTED (Book #5)
ONCE PINED (Book #6)
ONCE FORSAKEN (Book #7)
ONCE COLD (Book #8)
ONCE STALKED (Book #9)
ONCE LOST (Book #10)
ONCE BURIED (Book #11)
ONCE BOUND (Book #12)
ONCE TRAPPED (Book #13)
ONCE DORMANT (Book #14)
ONCE SHUNNED (Book #15)
ONCE MISSED (Book #16)
ONCE CHOSEN (Book #17)

MACKENZIE WHITE MYSTERY SERIES
BEFORE HE KILLS (Book #1)
BEFORE HE SEES (Book #2)
BEFORE HE COVETS (Book #3)
BEFORE HE TAKES (Book #4)
BEFORE HE NEEDS (Book #5)
BEFORE HE FEELS (Book #6)
BEFORE HE SINS (Book #7)
BEFORE HE HUNTS (Book #8)
BEFORE HE PREYS (Book #9)
BEFORE HE LONGS (Book #10)
BEFORE HE LAPSES (Book #11)
BEFORE HE ENVIES (Book #12)
BEFORE HE STALKS (Book #13)
BEFORE HE HARMS (Book #14)

AVERY BLACK MYSTERY SERIES
CAUSE TO KILL (Book #1)
CAUSE TO RUN (Book #2)
CAUSE TO HIDE (Book #3)
CAUSE TO FEAR (Book #4)
CAUSE TO SAVE (Book #5)
CAUSE TO DREAD (Book #6)

KERI LOCKE MYSTERY SERIES
A TRACE OF DEATH (Book #1)

A TRACE OF MURDER (Book #2)
A TRACE OF VICE (Book #3)
A TRACE OF CRIME (Book #4)
A TRACE OF HOPE (Book #5)

PROLOGUE

Lisa had only consumed one glass of wine, but the feeling of heaviness as she lay in front of her TV in the living room was like nothing she'd ever experienced.

It had been a long day, sure; her job as a lawyer tended to suck the life out of her more often than not, but she usually finished up with a glass of wine--sometimes three--as she watched her favorite soaps. This time, she was struggling to keep her eyes open on the hazy TV screen before her, cutting into the darkness of her living room.

She resisted the pull of sleep. It was just too early, and besides, she didn't want to miss what would happen next on screen. She'd waited all week for this episode to air, and she smiled dreamily at the characters on the TV as they made jokes. She sat upright and took another sip of wine. Maybe that would wake her up.

But the wine wasn't working. It was as if the heaviness inside her was pulling her down, making her feel like she was sinking. Lisa tried to shake it off, but the more she moved, the more it seemed to take hold.

She tried to push herself up off the couch, but her limbs felt like they were made of lead. Panic set in as she realized something was definitely not right. The room started spinning, and her vision blurred. She could barely keep her eyes open.

As she fought to keep awake, she saw a shadowy figure enter the room.

Lisa jolted awake to a bright screen in front of her.

For a moment, she was sure she was still on her couch, and it had all been a dream. But the room that materialized around her wasn't her living room--not at all.

It was a long, narrow room with a projector screen, like a small movie theater built just for her.

And she couldn't close her eyes. Or move her head.

Panic set in as Lisa glanced down at both of her arms, clasped to the chair, forcing her still.

She struggled and tugged, trying to break free, but the restraints held tight. Her eyes darted around the room, searching for anything that could help her escape. But there was nothing--just that screen in front of her, playing fuzzy white noise.

"H-Help!" Lisa managed to scream, but her throat was bone dry. She could feel her pulse increasing as the fear moved through her veins.

This couldn't be real.

It couldn't be happening.

And yet she couldn't wake up. All she could see was this room with this blank white projector screen.

Then, a ticking sound.

The screen went dark, before light bloomed back to life. On the screen, a countdown from three, two, one...

An image on the screen. An animal, a lion running after its prey.

Guts. Limbs being ripped apart.

Then insects. Flies, swarming what looked to be flesh.

Lisa could feel her stomach churn as she watched the screen in front of her. Her eyes shifted, wide and terrified. She felt her heart pounding in her chest, her pulse racing, sweat beginning to bead on her brow.

Her breathing grew quicker, and she felt lightheaded. They're just images, she told herself, but she couldn't help it. She was terrified. Whatever this was, it was one of the most realistic things she had ever seen, and the thought of what she was watching began to plague her mind.

More images. She couldn't look away.

A car crash, the screeching of brakes, then the impact, bodies flying around the inside of a crunched car.

A woman, running down a street as a gunshot rang in the distance.

She felt her chest tighten as her heart raced.

Screams, and a flash of light.

Another flash, and another. Lisa could feel her body begin to tense up, her stomach churning with sickness. She didn't know what was happening to her, but her heart--it was pounding louder and louder by the second, so loud and heavy she was sure it would punch its way out of her chest wall.

She was barely conscious of the images on screen. They seemed to blur, but then she was aware of something else. A burning in her stomach.

Burning.

And it was spreading to her arms, her legs, her chest.

She was burning on the inside, and she felt like she was going to be sick.

The pain was intense. She could feel herself breaking out into a sweat, her stomach churning. Her body was shaking uncontrollably.

And then the images began to slow down.

They started to stretch out, like the projector was rewinding.

She froze as she watched herself inside the screen.

The pain was almost unbearable.

It was as if she were watching every moment of her life flash by, in reverse.

It was going to rip her apart, she thought.

Her heart beat louder and louder and pain shot through her arm. She went dizzy. She couldn't close her eyes, and yet her vision blurred into a haze of those awful images.

Then, with one last squeeze in her heart, everything went black.

CHAPTER ONE

Special Agent Morgan Cross of the FBI stared down the barrel of a gun, pointed at her face in the front doorway of her house. The culprit: Darren La Roux, an ex-con she'd helped put behind bars years ago, before Morgan's own ten-year stint in prison. He'd been put down as an accomplice to murder, a bystander who had known his brother was killing people, and even turned a blind eye to it happening in their own home. Morgan remembered thinking his chance of parole was total crap—but he must have gotten out on good behavior.

She didn't have time to think. Her life flashed before her eyes, and her instincts kicked into high gear. First, she ducked as Darren fired a shot into her house in a deafening bang that was meant for her.

Then she smacked his arm, hitting him in the perfect spot to disarm him. His gun flew off to the side, landing somewhere in her front garden, and Morgan immediately wrestled Darren, grabbing onto his strong arms with both of hers. The nighttime air surrounded them, but with a resounding push, Darren shoved Morgan back into her house.

She had a gun in here, of course, but it was nowhere within her reach.

She stumbled onto the floor and looked up as Darren slammed the door behind him, trapping them both inside, looking down at her, crazed like a hungry animal. He had a spider tattoo across his skull now, his hair shaved short, his stocky frame more menacing than she remembered.

"How the hell are you here?" she shouted, standing on shaky legs.

Darren stared at her with cold eyes, his breaths coming out in ragged gasps. "I'm here for revenge, Cross. You put me in prison, and now it's time for you to pay for what you did to me."

Morgan's heart raced as she tried to calculate her next move. She could see the anger and hatred in Darren's eyes, and she knew he wouldn't hesitate to kill her. She needed to stay calm and find a way out of this.

"I did my job," she said, her voice steady. "You were guilty of the crimes you were accused of, and you deserved to be punished."

Darren laughed bitterly. "Deserved to be punished? You ruined my life, Cross. You took everything from me."

Morgan took a step back, fists raised. Skunk, her elderly Pitbull, barked loudly at Darren, but Morgan shushed him.

"Maybe I should kill that mutt of yours first," Darren said.

She gritted her teeth. She couldn't let Darren kill Skunk.

"You want me? Then fine," Morgan said. "I'm right here. Leave the dog out of it."

"Sorry, Morgan," Darren said, his tone grim. "You should've taken me seriously before. Now you're gonna pay for it."

That's when she made her move. As Darren stepped forward, Morgan grabbed a vase off her coffee table and shattered it over his head. He stumbled back but, undeterred, he lunged forward and grabbed her, wrapping his hands around her neck. Skunk jumped at Darren and bit into his leg, and Darren kicked at Skunk, eliciting a whine of pain that broke Morgan's heart.

"Down, Skunk!" Morgan shouted.

The dog kept barking. Morgan had to get Darren the hell out of here. If they were going to fight, they'd have to do it outside.

"You want me, right, La Roux?" Morgan shouted. "Well come get me!"

Without another word, Morgan scrambled through the kitchen, and Darren tore after her. Morgan darted out the back door, sprinting across her dark backyard. She looked back to make sure Darren was following.

He was.

His bulky frame chased after her.

A feeling of dread weighed down on her chest. What the hell was she going to do now?

Morgan's eyes darted back and forth, searching for anywhere safe to go. Ahead of her, her neighbor's light illuminated their backyard, and Morgan ran for it. As she reached the fence, she climbed over it and fell into the grass on the other side.

Morgan landed with a thud and rolled onto her back. Darren hopped after her, and Morgan tore around the side of the neighbor's house, to the empty street. It was late, and no one was out. Morgan couldn't risk getting anyone else involved in this--Darren was on a warpath, and she was sure he'd kill anyone who stood between him and Morgan.

So, Morgan kept running, leading him away, to the small commercial area just up the street, buildings with long alleyways.

"You can't escape me, Cross!" Darren shouted, and Morgan kept running. Her lungs heaved. Her legs were burning. But she wouldn't stop.

She couldn't.

As she raced through the alleyway, she found herself in a dead end. She stopped, looking around, searching for anything, anything she could use to protect herself.

"I'm right here, Cross," Darren said, his voice calm as he appeared at the end of the alleyway, a long and menacing shadow.

She was pinned against a wall, nowhere to go. But Darren was right there, ready to pounce.

Hand-to-hand, it was.

She had no choice but to fight. Without another thought, she threw her fist at him, and Darren blocked her easily. He backhanded her across the cheek, and Morgan stumbled back.

She caught her breath and threw another punch, and he caught that one, too, and slammed a fist against her cheek.

He was strong, and he was determined to make her pay for putting him in jail.

But so was she.

Morgan rallied her strength and threw a roundhouse kick at Darren's face, but he caught her ankle and pulled her forward. As she flew across the alleyway, Darren's momentum carried him forward, too. She tried to scramble away, but he was smarter than she'd given him credit for. He was like a rabid dog, catching her by the waist and slamming her against the brick wall.

She struggled against him, but Darren's grip was strong and determined.

Then he lunged at her, grabbing her by the throat. She dropped to the ground, and Darren fell on top of her, straddling her. His hands around her neck tightened, and Morgan clawed at Darren's hands to make him let go.

"Say goodbye to the world, Cross," he said in a cold, detached voice.

With every ounce of strength that she had left, Morgan grabbed Darren's arms and shoved them to the side as hard as she could. She pushed upward with all her strength, effectively lifting Darren's weight. Darren lost balance, and his grip on her loosened.

He stumbled, losing his footing as he tripped backwards--right toward a metal dumpster in the alleyway.

Everything moved in a blur.

Darren fell back.

Morgan watched in horror as the back of his head smashed against the corner of the dumpster.

Darren fell with a thud, his body completely stiff.

The shadow of his body fell over Morgan, and she rolled over, catching her breath.

No movement.

No sound.

Darren was motionless.

Morgan sat up and caught her breath, staring at him. His face was completely still.

She kept waiting for him to move, but he didn't.

Slowly, she reached out and placed a hand against Darren's cheek, then checking for a pulse. His body was still warm, but as blood pooled around him, Morgan felt zero pulse.

He was dead.

Morgan snatched her hand away and scrambled to her feet. She stepped back, shaking.

No, no, no.

It was happening again.

Morgan had just been released from prison after ten years behind bars, arrested wrongfully. She was still getting to the bottom of what had happened--she had been working a case, and there may have been an undercover agent nearby, someone who had reported her for something she never did.

She'd lost ten years of her life. She missed out on most of Skunk's life. She'd missed chances to progress her career, to fall in love, to start a family.

She'd missed her father's death.

She hadn't even been able to attend his funeral.

She couldn't go back.

But how could she explain this?

An ex-con had tried to kill her, and now he was dead in an alleyway. There were no witnesses. No one to corroborate her innocence in this.

She could be charged with murder.

Again.

But she wanted to do things right. She had to call it in, to tell someone, but what if they didn't believe her? She had to come up with a proper gameplan, a way to do it right and—

Suddenly, the sound of footsteps scuffling. Someone was coming.

Morgan didn't think.

She just ran.

On instinct, she tore through the alleyway and out into the street; then she kept running, hopping over people's fences, and tearing through their backyards until she reached her own. The whole thing felt like a dream—or a nightmare.

She darted in through the back door, and closed it behind her, locking it. She threw the deadbolt and then the chain. Then she shut and locked the front door, too.

With the doors secured, she took a deep breath and let herself relax a little. Skunk walked up to her and nuzzled her with his nose, and Morgan quickly checked him for injuries. He seemed fine, just shaken up from when Darren had kicked him.

Morgan sank to the floor and wrapped her arms around the dog.

Morgan had been wrong all along. She wasn't safer now that she was free from prison.

She was far from safe.

There was the idea that a fellow agent had potentially betrayed her and had her sent to prison.

Now, she had even more questions.

Why had Darren come for her now?

How had he even found her?

And why the hell did she run? By the time she realized what she'd done, it was too late, and she'd fled the crime scene, making her look bad. She couldn't tell anyone now. If she did, they wouldn't believe her for sure; but in the moment, when she'd heard someone coming, it was instinct that caused her to run.

She couldn't go back to prison. She couldn't risk putting her trust in people either because what had that gotten her before? Ten years behind bars. But she had to do something.

These questions plagued Morgan as she sat in her living room, with Skunk at her feet and her head in her hands. She couldn't trust anyone with this. Not even her partner, Derik Greene.

No one could know what happened here tonight.

CHAPTER TWO

Morgan was numb. She didn't know how much time had passed as she sat on the floor, simply holding Skunk, before she pulled herself up.

She had to keep living. Like nothing had happened.

Maybe nothing really had happened. It all felt surreal.

"Wanna go for a walk, boy?" she asked Skunk as she steadied herself on shaky legs.

Skunk hopped up and gave her big eyes, whining.

"C'mon," Morgan said, "let's go for a walk. We could both use some fresh air."

Morgan grabbed her keys from the table by the door, then put Skunk on the leash. She headed out, locking the door behind her, and stepped into the cool night. Hazy clouds had rolled in, blocking out the stars.

She didn't need to go far. Just for a little walk.

She kept her mind clear and tried to just think of nothing. Just the steady rhythm of her footsteps against the pavement and Skunk's paws.

Just keep in motion.

She squeezed her eyes shut, and the memory of Darren's dead body flashed in her mind.

Morgan opened her eyes again. She tried to stop thinking, but it was impossible.

As they walked, she thought about everything that had happened-- how she'd gone from being free to being in jail, and how she'd lost ten years. Now, she was free again.

But now her father was dead.

She felt even smaller and more depressed than she had in prison, a feeling she hadn't even experienced until she'd gotten out. Now, she felt like she'd done nothing with her life. She knew it wasn't true; she had put many criminals behind bars. But at the same time, what good would it do if they could just get released from jail and come after her years later?

She shuddered as Skunk stopped to sniff a tree. She zoned out on the lawn of one of her neighbor's houses. Images of cold cell walls, bars, and other inmates swam through her mind.

She couldn't go back to prison.

She was only forty. Still young enough to have a normal life. But if she lost another ten years? She'd be fifty. She'd grow old knowing so many years had been wasted.

There was no way she was going to spend the rest of her life behind bars.

No way.

But what she'd done with Darren--it had been the worst possible way to handle that. And now, here she was, walking her dog like nothing had happened.

"Hey, Morgan!" someone said, and Morgan's eyes snapped to one of her neighbors, Jason, walking his small dog. She had seen him a few times since she moved back.

Morgan's hair stood on end. Jason was smiling at her, but she wanted nothing to do with him, not right now. Paranoid thoughts racked her brain.

Maybe he'd seen Darren come to Morgan's house.

Maybe he knew what happened.

Jason's lips began to move, words coming from his mouth that went in one of Morgan's ears and out the other. She was still in a daze, still partially in that alleyway. She was hoping that, somehow, she had made this whole night up.

Skunk's bark pulled her from her reverie. Jason was frowning at her.

"Are you okay, Morgan?"

She snapped out of it. "I'm fine. Sorry, I—I have to go."

Feeling out of her body, Morgan turned and walked away, leaving Jason and his dog in the street.

Morgan didn't lose her cool often, but clearly, she was still in shock. She wanted—no, *needed*—to be alone.

When she got home, she let Skunk into the house, then she slid the extra deadbolt into place. She glanced out the window and saw Jason walking past her house with his dog, on his way home. He shot her house a disapproving look before he kept going.

Overwhelmed, Morgan headed upstairs to her bedroom. She went inside and locked that door, too, then looked around the room.

The room didn't feel like hers. It was too quiet and too big.

She'd lived in a cell for ten years. She hadn't even had a bed or a real mattress. She'd slept on a hard metal cot. She was used to small rooms. She'd been stripped of her belongings at the warden's office.

She'd been forced to wear prison-issued clothing--a jumpsuit and white cotton shoes--every day.

She'd been surrounded by some of the hardest women imaginable, and so Morgan had to harden herself too.

To be more than an FBI agent, but to fit in there as a criminal.

A criminal.

If there was any doubt that she was one before, she definitely was now. She had willingly left the body in an alleyway. It was criminal negligence at best, manslaughter at worst. She hadn't meant to kill Darren, but he'd fallen back and hit his head, and it had all happened so fast.

She should have called the police or the FBI or at least Derik, right then and there. Deal with it by the books. She'd acted in self-defense, and she was an FBI agent, for Christ's sake.

But after what happened to her, when she was wrongfully convicted, she'd lost faith in the system she was still a slave to.

So, she ran. And walked her dog, in a hazy state of shock.

And hadn't considered the ramifications of what she'd done.

All she'd done was think about herself, and how she felt.

And she wasn't ready to face what she'd done. Not yet.

Maybe she should just leave. Leave the country. Leave the FBI, leave it all behind.

She could get a new name, a new life. New friends, a new home.

Her mind was exhausted, and her body was still on edge; she was nervous and angry and confused, things were happening too fast, and she had to get a grip. But she was at a loss for control.

Where could she go from here? Maybe some pills would help, something to calm the nerves. Then again, maybe drugs were the last thing she needed right now.

She decided to shower. Maybe that would help. Maybe she would feel better after.

She went into the ensuite bathroom and turned on the hot water.

She stripped down, kicked off her shoes, and watched her clothes sink to the floor. Then, she stepped into the warm shower, feeling the steam take over her senses.

She thought about everything again. She'd killed a man.

She was a murderer.

It wasn't the same as when she'd had to kill on duty.

This had been different.

She'd been angry and scared and ready to lash out. No matter how much she tried to justify her actions, she knew that's what had happened. Even if it was self-defense, there was no one there to back her up.

She stood under the showerhead and slowly relaxed. Her mind became less scrambled and she was able to think more clearly.

She had to face this, whatever it was.

She needed to tell the FBI what she'd done.

If Morgan knew anything, it was that these things had a way of coming back to bite.

But she couldn't bring herself to do it. She couldn't even bring herself to turn off the shower.

It was a hard decision because she knew she had to do it. She was going to tell someone. She just didn't know who.

Derik?

He'd believe her, at least. He'd understand. He'd help her, at least.

She hoped he would, anyway.

And even if he did help her, what if it got him fired? Derik had always been more by the books than Morgan was. Maybe she couldn't trust him with this, after all.

She closed her eyes and waited until the water ran cold.

When she turned off the water and opened the shower door, she was completely numb.

She dried off and wrapped a towel around herself, then she went back into the bedroom and collapsed on the bed, closing her eyes.

She didn't know how long she was out, but exhaustion took over and she was asleep, dreaming of cold cell walls and pools of blood over concrete.

***

Morgan awoke with a start, her phone vibrating on her nightstand beside her bed. Her room was full of darkness, but with a sliver of blue through the curtains from the early morning light. Her clock read six a.m.

Memories of last night pooled in like acid. None of it felt real: the gun in her face, Darren, the fight in the alleyway.

Trying not to think about it, she grabbed her phone and answered it.

"Hello?" she said.

"Are you okay?" Derik asked.

"What?"

"I've been trying to call you for an hour. I got worried. I was about to head over there."

Morgan's breath caught. She hadn't even realized. It wasn't like her to not wake up for a call.

"I'm sorry," she said. "I fell asleep."

"I thought something happened. You weren't answering your phone. I was on my way over to your house. I was worried."

"No, it's fine," she said. "I'm fine."

"Are you sure? It's not like you to skip a call, and last night--"

"I just fell asleep is all," she said. "I'm sorry."

In the shower last night, Morgan had considered telling Derik the truth. But now that she heard his voice, she knew there was no way she could do that. Not a chance. She and Derik were just building back their partnership, and even though he'd believed her once before, would he believe her a second time? The thought of confessing, of trying to get him on her side, terrified her.

But why was Derik calling her now?

"What's going on, anyway?" Morgan asked. "I know you didn't just call to check on me."

"Yeah, right, I..." He sighed. "I just got off the phone with Director Mueller. We need to meet at HQ. There's a case."

Morgan sat up in her bed. After everything that had happened, it sounded impossible to just slip back into work as if nothing had even changed. She remembered the way she'd ignored at her neighbor last night.

Could she handle work today?

"Can you meet me there within fifteen?" Derik asked. "Or do you need me to pick you up?"

Morgan's head pounded, completely put on the spot. But she didn't want to end up stranded without her car. "I'll drive myself in, no worries."

"Let's meet by the elevators."

Morgan looked at the clock. "I'll be there in ten."

"See you then."

She hung up the phone and simply stared at it for a moment. In the last twenty-four hours, she'd talked to Derik about their feelings for each other, finished a case, then had a man try to kill her--and killed him in return.

And now, she had to go to work.

She wasn't sure she could do it.

But she had to. If she didn't, she'd only look suspicious.

So, sucking in her dignity, Morgan quickly got ready for the day and headed out, hoping the weight of this secret wouldn't eat her alive.

CHAPTER THREE

Morgan walked through the FBI parking lot, keeping her head low. The rain had picked up, and now it was falling hard, making her cold. She was dressed in her best suit pants and blazer, attempting to mask how she felt inside by looking sharp on the outside. But she couldn't stop her nerves from being on high alert as she went in the building.

She reached the front of the building and went inside, shielded from the cool rain. Derik was already waiting for her at the elevator, and he stood at attention when Morgan saw him.

Her stomach twisted. How was she supposed to face him after what happened?

"Hey," Derik said, "thanks for coming in."

Morgan forced a small smile as she got closer. She tried to hide her face from him as she pressed the elevator button. Darren had landed some good hits on her, and she'd tried to cover the marks with makeup, but there was only so much she could do for swelling. And Derik had just seen her last night.

Morgan almost felt safe as she stepped into the elevator with Derik. But once the doors closed, he faced her with concern all over his expression. "Hey, what happened? You get into a bar fight after I left last night?"

He gestured at her face. "And your cheek is bruised. Did someone hit you?"

Morgan's heart raced, but she tried to keep her voice calm. "I'm fine."

"You look like shit."

"I'm fine, really," Morgan said. "Just...a long night. I tripped and hit my face on my bookshelf, and I'm not really proud of it so we don't have to talk about it."

She took a step back, trying to distance herself.

Derik was still moving closer. "It looks like a lot of bruising. Are you hurt? Do we need to get you to the ER?"

"I'm fine. I just hit the corner hard," she said.

Derik nodded, but his gaze was still searching.

The elevator stopped on the third floor and the doors opened. "It's fine," Morgan said. "I'll take care of it later."

She stepped off the elevator and turned left to head to her desk, but Derik grabbed her arm. "Are you sure you're alright?"

Morgan turned and looked him in the eye. She wanted to tell him everything. "I said I'm fine. It's nothing, okay? I fell. Nothing happened. Let it go."

Derik studied her for another few seconds. "Alright," he said. "Well, come with me to my office--I'll quickly brief you on this case, then we need to head out."

The back of Morgan's throat itched, but she didn't say anything. She followed after him, keeping her hands in her pockets so he couldn't see how she was shaking.

Derik's office was a lot like Morgan's, with a wooden desk and a plethora of papers stacked on it. He sat down in his desk chair and gestured for Morgan to sit on the other side. She tried to shove her anxiety aside and focus on the prospect of a case.

"So, here's what we have." Derik tossed her a folder, and Morgan flipped it open. In it were several glossy photographs--the first of a woman's body sitting, strapped to a chair, her head limp. Clearly deceased.

She appeared to be in a warehouse of some kind. And yet she was the only one there. Her eyes were also taped open, like she'd been forced to watch something.

"What the hell is this?" Morgan muttered.

She flipped through the next photos. More angles of the girl, then photos from the setting as well. Pictures of a projector screen in a long, narrow room.

"She died of a heart attack," Derik said.

Morgan turned the pictures around and looked at the woman's face. The way her eyes were forced open, but lifeless, was unnerving.

"Who is she?" Morgan asked.

"Lisa Fitzpatrick," Derik said. "She was a lawyer. Thirty-five."

Morgan mulled over the facts. If she died of a heart attack, it was possible this wasn't an intentional murder. A kidnapping, clearly, but not necessarily murder. It was disturbing, but she failed to see why it was on the FBI's desk and not in the hands of the police.

"Any reason why we're on this case?" Morgan asked.

"I figured you'd ask that," Derik said, standing, "which is why I think we should head out now, and we can see for ourselves. This woman was found last week. They just found another one this morning."

"Damn," Morgan said, standing too. "What are we waiting for?"

***

Derik's car felt like a cage. No matter how much Morgan tried to relax and think of this as just a regular case, it didn't feel like it. She fidgeted as he drove them toward the crime scene, through the dreary morning light.

She tapped her thumb nail against her teeth, then caught herself doing it and stopped. Then she sat on her hands to try to stop. Derik must have noticed, because he glanced at her and said, "Cross, are you sure you're good? You're not normally this anxious."

She took out her hands and crossed her arms, trying to appear nonchalant. "Fine. Just tired."

"That injury have anything to do with it?" Derik asked. "If you hit your head that hard, we really should get it checked out."

"I said I'm okay." Morgan couldn't help but snap at him. His concern was getting to her. "I'm just tired. And I'm coming off of one murder case and onto another, so yeah, if I'm a little on edge, it's only natural."

"Sorry," Derik said, "I just don't like seeing you hurt."

Morgan shook her head, her hair coming out of her ponytail and getting in her eyes. She was about to tell him to just drop it, but then she looked over at him, and was struck by how handsome the man was.

Derik's eyes were locked on the road, but his face was slightly flushed, his lips tight together, and his dark hair was combed to the side. She remembered how, recently, they'd kissed, and even more recently, they'd agreed to keep their relationship professional. The fact that he was showing care for her wasn't helping her drop the feelings for him. But even with all this, Morgan still didn't want to put what had truly happened on him.

She couldn't.

It was too risky.

For all of them.

18

Morgan turned her attention to the world outside the car. She'd been expecting a warehouse district, since the other victim had died somewhere like that, but this was looking more domestic. Suburban homes with trim lawns.

"Where are we going?" Morgan asked.

"Victim's house," Derik said.

"So, it's a change in MO."

"You'll see soon enough."

Morgan took a deep breath. She really wanted to believe things were okay and that it was just the stress finally getting to her, but something felt off here.

Derik turned down a residential street and parked on the curb. There was a house swarming with police officers and FBI personnel. A small one-story house with a white picket fence, a few well-maintained flower beds, and a barbecue grill on the front lawn. Domestic, if not for the officers. A young girl in an FBI jacket stormed out of the front door and fell to her hands and knees onto the grass, retching like she was going to vomit.

Morgan scowled. What were they about to find in here?

She traded a look with Derik, and he had the same grim expression. With no more time to waste, they got out of the car and headed up the lawn, moving past the girl and others with their badges out to identify themselves. They stepped inside the house, and Morgan found herself surrounded by a completely ordinary home. The interior of the house was homey and inviting. The walls were a soft pastel blue, with white furniture and polished hardwood floors. A cozy armchair in one corner, a bookcase full of books in another, a few family photos displayed on the mantle above the fireplace. Everything seemed to be in its proper place, as if nothing had been disturbed.

And yet, clearly, something sinister had happened here. Morgan held her breath, anticipating it.

Derik walked up to a grim-faced officer and said, "Where can we find the body?"

The officer nodded toward a door that led down into a basement. What struck Morgan more was that downstairs, there were lights flashing as though a TV were on.

"What's going on down there?" Morgan asked.

"We left everything undisturbed, as requested by Agent Greene," the officer said, nodding at Derik. "The crime scene as just as it was, so you can go downstairs and see for yourselves. We've cleared the area."

Derik and Morgan exchanged glances, then headed down the stairs, into the eerie light of the basement. As Morgan reached the bottom step, she looked over to see some sort of home theater--with a film playing on a projector screen.

Disturbing images flashed across the screen.

Animals hunting, sinking their teeth into bloody flesh.

Symbols.

Insects.

It all moved so fast, so chaotically, that Morgan couldn't even keep up.

"Jesus," Derik said.

Morgan's eyes snapped to a seat in front of the screen, where the body of a man was strapped in, much like the woman from the photograph.

His head was hanging down, face pale, his tongue lolling from his mouth.

Morgan stared, her breaths coming shallowly and rapidly. She'd seen bodies before, but she'd never seen anything like this. If the other incident with the woman didn't prove someone was killing these people, then this did.

Morgan felt a rage building in her chest. Whoever did this, they needed to pay.

"Why did they leave the film running?" Derik asked.

"Maybe they wanted to let the victim watch his own death," Morgan replied, "especially if they strapped him up like that." She nodded at the projector, clicking as it played the movie. "We need to take this film and get it analyzed, find out who made it."

"Agreed. It's damn freaky." Derik wandered over to the projector.

Morgan held her breath as he grabbed the film reel, expecting something terrible to happen. But to her relief, nothing happened--until a loud spark sizzled and the projector exploded in a violent shower of sparks.

The shockwave hit Morgan's face like a wall of heat, and she stumbled backwards, shielding her eyes with her arm. All around, there was an acrid smell of burning plastic and metal. The screen went dark, and smoke filled the air.

Derik rushed to turn off the projector, but it was too late; the damage had been done. They were both coughing from the thick cloud of smoke, their eyes stinging from the fumes. Morgan looked forward to see the remains of the film reel, completely destroyed.

CHAPTER FOUR

Morgan stood in the smoke and ashes of the wreckage as the team worked to salvage what they could. As she watched the scene unfold, officers and FBI personnel working together to retrieve evidence, everything that happened with Darren seemed to fade into the back of her mind.

This was just what she needed.

A case to distract herself.

And this one happened to intrigue her more than she had expected.

She turned to Derik who was standing beside her, his face grim. "What do we do now?" she asked, her voice barely audible over the commotion around them.

Derik shook his head. "We need to find out who made that film. It could be the key to solving this case."

Morgan nodded, her mind already racing with possibilities. "Right. Except our evidence just combusted in front of us. Any chance the film was salvaged from the first crime scene?"

"I wish it had been," Derik said. "It was destroyed. I guess we didn't discuss that part."

Morgan nodded, agreeing with him. "But who would do something like this?" she wondered aloud. "And why?"

"Someone sick, no doubt."

Morgan's focus drew to the body, which was still strapped in place. She got a closer look. The man was likely in his early forties, a different MO from the original victim. Lisa had been in her early thirties and a lawyer. Morgan didn't have all the details on this latest victim, but judging by this nice house, he had a high-paying job.

But at the moment, what intrigued her more wasn't who he was, but how he had died.

Lisa had died of a heart attack, Derik had said. This guy didn't have any visible injuries--so did he have a heart attack too?

How would the killer induce a natural death like that?

Morgan got closer to the body and took out her flashlight, shining a spotlight across his form. The restraints and forced-open eyes made her stomach roil, but she pushed on. The man wasn't of a small stature. Morgan wondered how the killer had come into the man's own house and overpowered him, forcing him into this chair.

Was he drugged?

An idea formed in Morgan's head. Maybe there was more evidence somewhere, a drink, something the killer could have used to incapacitate him. If that were the case, she wondered what the pathology of this killer was. Why would he want to show people this strange imagery? It brought her back to stories of mind control, experiments on the human psyche. She wondered if this was some sort of experiment, or if it all came back to one man just wanting to torture people in his own twisted way.

She breezed past Derik, toward the stairs. "I'm going to check the house."

Starting with the kitchen.

Derik didn't object as Morgan slipped past the personnel and went back upstairs. Daylight poured in through the windows, brightening the house.

Morgan took a deep breath and tried to compose herself before entering the kitchen. It looked just as ordinary as the rest of the house, with a gleaming granite countertop and stainless-steel appliances. Nothing seemed amiss, but Morgan knew that appearances could be deceiving. She began to rummage through the cabinets, looking for any signs of a struggle or any indication that the killer had been there. The kitchen was spotless, with no signs of a struggle or a break-in.

She opened the fridge and found nothing out of the ordinary. But as she was about to close the fridge, her eyes caught something strange. A bottle of water had a slight discoloration at the bottom. She picked it up and unscrewed the cap.

Inside, she found a small powdery residue, almost like ground-up pills.

Bingo.

She took a swab from her kit, carefully collected the powder, and sealed it before heading back to the basement. Derik was standing outside the room, his arms crossed.

"Find anything?" he asked.

Morgan nodded, showing him the sealed swab. "This was in the fridge. Looks like someone drugged our victim."

Derik's eyes glinted. "We need to get this analyzed, ASAP." He waved over a young forensics worker with an FBI lanyard around her neck. The girl trotted over, and Morgan saw it was the same girl who had thrown up on the lawn earlier. It seemed she'd recovered. "Take this to the lab and call us with the results ASAP," Derik said. "It's important. We want this information expedited."

The girl nodded, clearly eager to get away from this crime scene, and rushed up the stairs.

"Nice find, Cross," Derik said.

Morgan nodded, turning away, hands in her pockets. She watched as the rest of the crew kept working. "Find anything out about the identity of the victim?" she asked Derik.

"Yeah, his name is Mark Evans, forty-two," Derik replied. "He's a prominent counselor and therapist in the city, worked at one of the top practices. Single, no criminal record."

Morgan furrowed her brow. "Interesting. I wonder if there's a connection between him and Lisa. Who found him, anyway?"

"The police," Derik said. "His work called when he didn't show up; guess it's really not like him, so the cops came to do a wellness check. His door was left open, then they found him... like this. Called us right away."

"I see. And did Lisa's file mention who found her?"

"Yeah, some guy who went into the warehouse," Derik said.

"But the warehouse was abandoned," Morgan pointed out, her suspicion rising. "What was he doing there?"

Derik was quiet for a moment. "The police interviewed him."

"Excuse me," someone cut in, and they looked up to see a timid male officer approaching. He looked apprehensive as he said, "Sorry, but I couldn't help but overhear you were talking about the warehouse."

"That's right," Morgan said.

"I was on that case as well. I have to say, the other film was destroyed, but it was nothing like this. We actually thought the witness was the one who destroyed it."

Morgan frowned. For a second, she almost thought she's misheard him. "Sorry, what?"

"Well, it looked like it had been manually burned," the officer said. "And the witness had a lighter on him, and what looked like melted film on his shoe. He said it was just tar because he worked construction. I thought all of it was odd."

"Why wasn't this in the file?" Derik asked, hands on his hips.

The officer turned away. "I'm not sure. No one else seemed to agree with me, and at that time, we weren't sure what we were dealing with, so I guess that detail got lost."

Morgan's mind raced as she tried to piece together the puzzle. The witness at the warehouse was suspicious, and now with the discovery of the potentially drugged water in Mark Evans's fridge, it seemed like they were dealing with a serial killer who had a methodical way of incapacitating his victims. She wondered if there were any other connections between the victims. More than that, she wondered what this warehouse witness knew.

"Do you remember the witness's name?" she asked the officer.

The officer nodded. "Yeah, I do. It was... Aaron, Aaron Matthews."

Morgan made a mental note of the name. "Thank you for telling us this," she said to the officer.

"No problem," he said, before quickly walking away.

Morgan turned to Derik. "We need to find this Aaron Matthews. Something about him doesn't sit right with me."

Derik nodded in agreement. "Agreed. Let's head to the precinct and see what they have on him."

They both headed up, leaving Mark's house behind as they stepped back into the daylight. Morgan felt cold as she walked toward Derik's car, sliding into the passenger seat beside him. As Morgan buckled in, Derik turned on the car, and the sound of the radio filled the silence.

A baritone voice was in the middle of saying: "A former convict, recently released from prison, has been found dead."

Morgan's blood turned to ice.

She went to slap the radio off, but Derik was faster.

He turned it up.

Morgan froze, not daring to even breathe.

"Darren La Roux, forty-three, was found dead after being in a suspected altercation with an unknown person in an alleyway on the south end of the city. Police are looking into the matter and treating La Roux's death as suspicious."

Derik turned down the radio, and Morgan could breathe again, but only for a moment. His eyes fell on her, and she turned to stone.

"La Roux... Cross, didn't we put that guy away?"

Morgan took a breath. This was the one moment she had to keep it together.

"Yeah, we did," she said, brows pinching, feigning surprise. "I didn't know he was out."

"Really?" Derik asked. "You don't know anything about this?"

Morgan scowled. "Why the hell would I know something?" Her offense was honest, as she didn't know why Derik would immediately assume Morgan knew something about it.

Even if she had been the one to shove Darren off her last night, hurling him toward the dumpster where he smashed his head.

Derik's brows furrowed in contemplation, and for a moment, Morgan feared he would see through her lie. But then he sighed and shook his head. "Sorry. I don't know what came over me. It's just that La Roux was a dangerous man, and I wouldn't want him on the loose."

Morgan let out a breath she didn't know she was holding. "I know, Derik. But we did our jobs, and we put him away. Whatever happened to him isn't on us."

Derik nodded, but Morgan could see the worry etched on his face. The two of them had worked hard to take down La Roux, and he was someone they couldn't forget easily.

Apparently, he hadn't forgotten her, either.

But had he been planning on going after Derik too?

Morgan didn't know. All the answers died with Darren.

And now Morgan had just dug herself a deeper hole by lying directly to Derik about it.

As they drove to the precinct, Morgan couldn't help but feel the weight of guilt settling into her stomach. She knew she should have told Derik the truth about what happened with La Roux, but fear of the consequences had stopped her. She had acted on instinct, not thinking about the potential fallout.

"What are you thinking?" Derik's voice broke through her thoughts.

Morgan looked over at him, seeing the concern etched on his face. "Just trying to piece everything together," she said, her voice failing to mask the guilt she was feeling.

Derik nodded, his gaze returning to the road ahead of them. "We'll get to the bottom of this, don't worry," he said, trying to reassure her.

But he was trying to reassure her on the case, when Morgan was really torn up with guilt over Darren, yet again.

She had to push it aside, to focus on the case at hand.

But her mind kept drifting back to the memory of what she had done to La Roux. The way she had pushed him with so much force that he had gone crashing into the dumpster, the sound of his skull cracking off the metal.

She had to keep her secret, no matter what it took.

<h1 style="text-align:center">CHAPTER FIVE</h1>

As they arrived at the precinct, Morgan took a deep breath, trying to shake off the feeling of guilt that clung to her like a shroud. She and Derik stepped out of the car and made their way inside, heading straight for the detective's bullpen.

The precinct was bustling with activity, with officers rushing back and forth, phones ringing off the hook, and people shouting orders. Morgan and Derik navigated through the chaos, their eyes scanning the room for some direction, until Morgan spotted a tall man with a beige jacket on and a detective badge on his belt, talking to another officer. Apparently, the lead detective who had talked to Aaron after he found Lisa's body was a man named Detective Steven Stoll, and if Morgan had to guess, this was him.

They headed straight for him.

"Excuse me, Detective Stoll?" Morgan said, getting his attention.

The detective turned to face her, his eyes scanning her and Derik up and down. "Yes, can I help you?"

Morgan flashed her badge. "I'm Special Agent Morgan Cross, and this is Special Agent Derik Greene."

"We were hoping to get some information on the witness who found Lisa's body," Derik said, stepping forward.

Stoll's expression turned guarded. "Why do you need that information?"

Morgan spoke up. "We believe that this witness may have more information that could be useful to our investigation. As I'm sure you know, another body has been found, and the case has been handed to the FBI."

"Yeah, I heard." Stoll sighed, running a hand through his hair. "Look, I've already talked to the guy, and he didn't have anything useful to say."

"We'd like to talk to him too," Morgan said, unsure why Stoll was resisting. Then again, sometimes detectives or police could be difficult about the FBI coming in and taking over their cases. "And I'd like to know everything about him before we do, so if you could please brief us..."

Stoll sighed, then nodded. "All right. Come into my office."

Morgan and Derik followed Stoll into his office, where he sat down in his chair and motioned for them to take a seat across from him. Morgan took out a notepad and pen, ready to take notes.

"His name is Aaron Matthews," Stoll began. "He's an activist of some kind. I guess he and his friends were holding meetings and movie nights in the warehouse, and that was what had brought him there. We didn't find out much else about them."

Morgan frowned. "What do you mean movie nights? Why there?"

"Well, there was so much space, it was easy to project a screen there," Stoll said.

That was odd. The killer had apparently thought of that too.

Or already knew about it.

"You never tried to contact the group?" Morgan asked.

"We talked to them, but they all seemed like a fairly innocuous group of young people talking about social activism and local issues and all that." Stoll sighed. "Look, it's not my area of expertise. All I cared about was finding out what happened to that woman, and they all seemed to have alibis."

"Including Aaron Matthews?" Derik asked.

"Not for the night before, but the kid called it in. He seemed sincere, and we had no reason to hold him, especially considering the victim died of natural causes. We really couldn't prove that she hadn't gotten into that chair willingly, or even put herself there."

Morgan could hardly believe what she was hearing. "Why would she strap herself into a chair and force her own eyes open? How?"

Stoll glared at her. "I'm not saying she did it herself, I'm just saying we had no just cause to keep Aaron Matthews for more than twenty-four hours."

Morgan scribbled down the information. "Did he say anything about seeing anyone suspicious around the area?"

Stoll shook his head. "No, he didn't see anyone. He just found the body and called it in."

"Did he seem nervous or agitated when you talked to him?" Derik asked.

Stoll paused, thinking. "No, not particularly. He seemed shocked, of course, but not overly nervous or anything like that."

Morgan continued to take notes as they spoke, trying to piece together any information that could be useful. She definitely wanted to talk to Aaron herself, because right now, she wasn't trusting Stoll's judgement.

"And what about the destroyed film?" Morgan said.

"It was like that when Matthews found it," Stoll replied.

"So he claimed."

Stoll's expression hardened. "What are you saying? We interrogated him long and hard, Special Agent Cross."

"What about the spot on his boot?" Morgan fired back. "One of your own officers believed it to be part of a melted film reel, suggesting he may have destroyed it himself."

"It was tar, from his job," Stoll said.

"You tested it?" Morgan lifted a brow.

Once more, Stoll's face went red. "We did not."

Morgan's suspicion only grew stronger at Stoll's evasive responses. She knew she had to speak to Aaron Matthews herself, get a sense of whether or not he was telling the truth.

"It sounds like you could've gone a lot deeper with your investigation, Detective," Morgan said. "Why didn't you?"

Stoll's expression grew stony. "We had nothing to charge him with and nowhere else to go. We had no reason to hold him, so he left." Stoll's jaw clenched. "I did what I could."

Morgan could feel the tension rising between them, but she knew it wasn't the time to argue. She needed to keep a cool head and keep collecting information.

"Do you have an address?" Morgan asked.

Stoll nodded. "I'll give it to you."

Stoll scribbled the address down on one of the notepads on his desk and handed it to Morgan.

"We appreciate your cooperation, Detective Stoll," Morgan said evenly, rising from her seat. "We'll be sure to follow up on this information."

Stoll nodded, then gestured to the door. "Good. Now if you don't mind, I have a lot on my plate."

Derik rose as well. "Of course. Have a good day, Detective."

With that, Morgan and Derik exited Stoll's office and headed back out into the bullpen, full of officers going about their business.

Morgan glanced at the paper Stoll had given her, then pulled out her phone and began to locate the address on a map.

"So, what did you think of him," Derik asked.

Morgan took a deep breath. "To be honest, I'm not sure. He just seemed very defensive."

"Sometimes it's hard for people to admit they may have been wrong about someone," Derik said.

They made their way out of the precinct and towards the car. Once they were finally alone, Morgan let out a deep breath, feeling a headache coming on.

All that mattered now was getting to Aaron Matthews's house and talking to him themselves.

As they drove, Morgan couldn't help but feel a sense of unease. There were too many unanswered questions, too many loose ends. She couldn't shake the feeling that something was off with this case.

Whatever it was, she intended to find out.

***

The address led them out of the city and into the suburbs, where the houses were small, and the streets were quiet. The tiny house sat alone, tucked between two larger houses. Its yellow paint had faded and peeled away in some spots, and its windows were dark and clouded with grime. The lawn was overgrown, with weeds poking through patches of dirt, and the fence was broken in several places. There was a sense of neglect and disrepair that hung in the air.

"Nice place," Derik said, peering out the window.

Morgan felt a knot form in her stomach. She wasn't sure what to expect, but she knew they had to be careful.

They got out of the car and approached the front door. Morgan knocked twice, waiting for a response, but none came.

She knocked again, this time a little louder. Still no answer. She turned to Derik and shrugged, unsure of what to do now.

They stood there for what felt like an eternity, but still no one answered the door. Morgan stepped back, her shoulders slumping in frustration. It seemed they were at a dead end. If Aaron wasn't home, then they'd have to look for him.

Suddenly, a voice:

"Are you looking for Aaron?"

Morgan's eyes snapped to a woman who stood on the sidewalk. She was young, maybe in her early twenties, and had short, dyed hair and facial piercings.

"Yes, we are," Morgan said, turning fully toward the girl.

She held her hands together timidly. "He's not here. No one's seen him in days."

Morgan's heart picked up. "What do you mean? He hasn't been home?"

"No, or at work," she said.

Morgan and Derik walked up to the girl and met her on the sidewalk, flashing their badges. The girl didn't look wholly surprised.

"Ever since the warehouse thing," she said, "he's been missing. We all stopped going there, but..."

"You're part of that activist group?" Derik asked.

The girl nodded timidly. "I'm Stacy. I already talked to the police last week, after it happened. I'm Aaron's roommate."

Morgan raised her brows. Stoll hadn't mentioned a roommate.

"So, you can let us inside," Morgan said.

"Well, yeah," Stacy said. "Do you think Aaron's in trouble? I'm worried about his mental health."

"Why didn't you report him missing?" Morgan asked.

"Because he does this sometimes," Stacy said. "He goes off the grid. It's not unlike him to disappear, but honestly, another few days and I would have reported him missing for sure."

Morgan and Derik followed Stacy into the house, cautiously stepping over piles of clothes and other clutter. The air was thick with the smell of stale cigarettes and unwashed dishes. The place was a mess, with dirty dishes piled up in the sink and garbage overflowing from the trash can.

"Sorry about the mess," Stacy said, leading them into a small living room. "Aaron's not the tidiest person. Neither am I."

Morgan took a quick scan of the room. The couch was threadbare and stained, the TV was old and chunky, and the walls were covered in posters for various punk bands. There was a guitar in the corner, a few books scattered on a coffee table, and a half-empty bottle of whisky on the floor.

"Does Aaron have any enemies?" Morgan asked, taking a seat on the couch.

"Well, the group as a whole hasn't been very happy with him," Stacy said. "He's been known to get a little aggressive during protests when we're trying to keep a peaceful image."

Morgan furrowed her brows. "Aggressive? How so?"

"He's just, like, really passionate about the cause," Stacy said, fidgeting with her hands. "He'll get in people's faces and shout at them, and sometimes he'll even throw things."

Morgan leaned forward, her eyes fixed on Stacy. "Do you think he's capable of hurting someone?"

Stacy bit her lip, thinking it over. "Honestly, I don't know. I don't think he would, but he has a temper."

Morgan nodded, making a mental note of everything Stacy had said. "Do you know of any place he might go to when he disappears?"

Stacy shook her head. "No, he's never told me anything like that. He just...vanishes."

Morgan nodded, taking note of the information. "Has he ever mentioned any specific threats or conflicts?"

Stacy shook her head. "Not that I know of. He's been pretty withdrawn lately, though. Not really talking to anyone."

Morgan leaned forward, her eyes meeting Stacy's. "Has Aaron ever talked about anything that seemed...off? Like he was planning something?"

Stacy hesitated, biting her lip. "Well...he's been talking a lot lately about how the government is corrupt and how the system is rigged against us."

"But nothing that would suggest he wants to hurt anyone, like the woman in the warehouse," Derik said.

"Oh, God no," Stacy said. "If anything, Aaron seemed to think the government did that to that woman. He was really freaked out. He thought they were after him. I think that might be why he disappeared too. He has a lot going on in his head."

"So, you don't think he did it," Morgan said.

"Of course not!" Stacy exclaimed. "That just... wouldn't be like him. There was no cause in that, not at all."

Morgan thought on it. Maybe Stacy was right, but then again, if Aaron was trying to spread his own theory about the government or something, it was possible he had gone to extreme lengths to stage some sort of attack.

At the same time, Morgan didn't see the clear motivation either.

"Do you mind if we take a look in his room?" Morgan asked.

Stacy stood and nodded. They followed Stacy through a dimly lit hallway and up a flight of stairs until they reached a small bedroom.

"This is Aaron's room," Stacy said, stepping aside to let them in.

The room was small and cramped, with clothes and papers scattered all over the floor. The bed was unmade, and the sheets were stained. Morgan wrinkled her nose in disgust. It was clear that hygiene wasn't a priority for Aaron.

She turned her attention back to the room, scanning it for any clues that could help solve the case.

But despite the mess, there was nothing that seemed out of place or suspicious. No threatening letters, no weapons, and no evidence that Aaron was planning something sinister. It looked like he had just been living his life as usual without any hint of malice or ill intent. Morgan and Derik began a routine search anyway, but nothing came up.

Maybe Stoll had been right, after all.

But as Morgan was glancing over Aaron's desk, she spotted a notebook tucked beneath another stack of books. She slid it out, then flipped it open. It was a sketchbook, and inside, there were strange symbols drawn.

Symbols...

It reminded Morgan almost of the symbols from the film in Mark Evans's house. Not an exact match; these were more rounded, more like Celtic crosses and knots, whereas the symbols from the film, to Morgan's memory, seemed to be more angular, potentially religious.

It wasn't a direct admission of guilt, but it was worth noting. Morgan snapped some photos and asked Stacy, "Do you mind if I take this?"

Stacy shrugged. "Go ahead."

Morgan nodded, tucking it under her arm.

Even with this, they needed to find Aaron and talk to him themselves. But maybe they'd have more of a case if they could link either of the victims back to him.

Morgan stood up and stretched her legs, trying to work out the kinks from the cramped bedroom. "Thank you for your help, Stacy. If you hear from Aaron, will you let us know?"

"Of course," Stacy said, looking worried. "I hope he's okay."

Morgan nodded.

She did too.

CHAPTER SIX

A city-wide search was on for Aaron Matthews, but so far, Morgan had heard nothing from any of her teams.

Back in her office at the FBI, she and Derik had split apart for a midday break. Morgan had her lunch out on her desk, a simple bagel and cream cheese with a black coffee, while she continued her research on her computer.

With Aaron Matthews missing, she wasn't sure where else to go other than to look into the victims. If she could draw a connection between them--or anyone else--then they might have something to work with.

First, they had Lisa Fitzpatrick. Thirty-five. A lawyer, as Derik had said. Morgan took a bite of her bagel and washed it down with coffee as she clicked through everything the internet had to say about Lisa and her life.

It seemed she had a fairly normal career--except for one incident in which she'd received public backlash due to helping a public figure, one Dave Smith, get a reduced sentence after being charged with human trafficking. Smith was an internet celebrity with millions of followers, and Lisa had been his lawyer. It was the only high-profile case she'd worked, though, and it had been three years ago. Morgan wasn't sure the motive would still be relevant today.

Then again, Morgan had helped put Darren La Roux in prison over ten years ago, and he'd come back for her last night.

No.

She shook it away.

She couldn't let the bad thoughts in. She had to focus on the case.

So, she did.

Morgan looked into some of the victims of Smith's human trafficking ring, and saw there were less than four confirmed victims, and all had moved far away from the city. It seemed unlikely they had come for revenge, and it also wouldn't make sense for them to have gone after Mark.

Then again, she hadn't looked into Mark yet.

Moving past Lisa for now, Morgan opened up Mark Evans's file. Forty-two, a therapist at a prestigious practice. On paper, it seemed a man like him had no enemies.

But as Morgan read through some of his notes, something caught her eye. Mark had been working with a patient who had a history of violence and had recently been released from prison.

Morgan's interest was piqued. She read through the patient's file, taking note of the man's history via the FBI database. His name was Michael Johnson, and he had been in and out of prison for most of his life. He had a history of violent outbursts and had been diagnosed with several mental illnesses.

Mark's notes indicated that Michael had begun canceling sessions, but of course, everything else was confidential.

Morgan sat back, sipping her coffee.

Could it be possible that Michael had killed Mark as an act of revenge for something that had happened in their sessions?

She looked in the database for anything that could link Lisa to any case Michael had ever been involved in, but she came up with nothing.

There was still no link between Mark and Lisa.

Morgan thought on it. There would be no information online or in the database, but someone in the office could talk, with the right motivation. It was hard to get people to break confidentiality, but when there were lives on the line and the FBI was involved, sometimes Morgan could get through.

Morgan decided to pay a visit to Mark's practice, hoping to find someone who would be willing to talk. She grabbed her jacket and headed out the door, making her way to the upscale office building in the heart of the city.

***

The practice where Mark Evans had worked clearly catered to a wealthy clientele, which didn't surprise Morgan, considering Mark's house had been fairly nice. Inside, the waiting room had plush furniture and expensive artwork on the walls. The receptionist was dressed impeccably, her desk spotless and shining with a computer monitor and sleek modern phone.

Morgan walked right up to the desk, taking note of how surprisingly empty the waiting area was. There was only one woman there, watching as Morgan approached the receptionist.

The receptionist looked up, her dark red hair tied back in a tight bun. "May I help you?"

Morgan flashed her FBI badge, and the woman's eyebrows shot up. Her nametag read "Eve."

"Good afternoon, Eve," Morgan said. "I was hoping to talk to you about Mark Evans."

Morgan glanced down the hall, noting that there were two doors. One said Dr. Carmichael.

The other had no nameplate at all.

Where was Mark Evans's nameplate? According to his file, he had been employed here.

And the receptionist clearly knew who he was because her face reddened with shock. "U-um, Dr. Evans isn't in right now."

"Of course not," Morgan said. Mark Evans was dead. But the news had clearly not spread. Morgan took a deep breath; maybe now wasn't the best time to drop this, but at the same time, she needed to push forward with the investigation—before more people lost their lives. So she said, "I'm sorry to tell you this, but he passed away."

Eve covered her mouth, stifling a gasp. "W-what?"

"I'm sorry to deliver this news," Morgan said, "but it's very important that I understand exactly what Mark Evans's position here was, to sort out if he had any enemies."

"Are you saying he was murdered?" Eve said through another gasp.

The woman in the waiting room stirred. Morgan glanced over at her, then focused on Eve, keeping her voice down.

"I can't confirm that," Morgan said, "I'm just trying to figure out what happened to him."

"Well, I'm sorry, but Dr. Evans actually didn't work here anymore."

"What?" Morgan scowled. "His file said he was presently employed."

Eve turned away. "It's... recent."

"Did something happen?"

Eve clammed up, averting her eyes. "No, of course not. He just wanted to move on."

"Then why wouldn't it be on his record? He didn't get another job."

Eve shook her head, clearly uncomfortable. "I can't discuss that with you. Dr. Evans was a private man, and I'm not permitted to give away any details of the practice. It's highly confidential."

Morgan took a deep breath, trying to hide her frustration. "I understand that, but please understand the gravity of this situation. The FBI doesn't come around just for fun, Eve. This is serious."

Eve looked away, saying nothing.

Morgan sighed. "I understand he had a patient named Michael Johnson."

Eve's eyes flashed. "I'm sorry, ma'am, but I'm not allowed to discuss any of this. I could lose my job."

Morgan leaned in closer, her voice low. "Look, Eve, I get it. Confidentiality is important. But someone killed Mark Evans. And if you know something, anything, that could help us figure out who did it, then it's your duty to tell me."

Eve hesitated, looking at Morgan with a mix of fear and determination. Finally, she spoke in a hushed voice. "I can't tell you much. All I can say is Michael stopped coming, and he wasn't the only patient that Dr. Evans lost."

Morgan hesitated. She had been thinking Michael was the suspect, but the way Eve had worded that--it sounded like Mark was the problem.

"Hold on," Morgan said, "are you implying that Dr. Evans had issues with more than one patient?"

Eve's face was now as red as her hair. "I'm sorry, ma'am, I can't tell you anything else. Please, I have to ask you to leave, unless you have a warrant or whatever it is you need to make this official."

Morgan sighed. She understood the girl's frustration and didn't want to push it.

"All right then," Morgan said. She took out a card and left it on the counter. "If you change your mind, or if anything comes up at all, please don't hesitate to call me."

Morgan walked out of the practice, deep in thought. There was more to this than she had initially thought. Mark Evans had clearly been dealing with some serious issues with patients, and it was possible that one of them had something to do with his death. But who? And why?

Morgan couldn't shake the feeling that there was something off about this case. She had a gut feeling that Mark's death was not a simple act of revenge or even a random act of violence.

There was something deeper going on here. She needed Derik's thoughts on this, so as she got in the elevator, she gave him a ring. Standing alone in the elevator, she pressed her phone to her ear and waited for Derik to pick up.

"This is Special Agent Greene," he eventually said, just as the elevator hit the bottom floor. Morgan stepped out, her heels clacking on the tile of the building as she made her way toward the exit.

"Greene, it's Cross," she said. "Where are you? I have a potential lead."

"Yeah, I have some info for you too," Derik said.

"Coffee?"

"Sounds good. Usual place?"

A smile crept on to Morgan's lips.

Before she'd gone to prison, she and Derik had a special café downtown where they had often met up during cases.

"Sounds good," she said, her heart warm. "See you soon."

They hung up. Now wasn't the time to feel good about anything, but Morgan couldn't help but look forward to sitting in that café with Derik again.

Morgan got in her car and drove toward the café. She had a feeling that this would be a long, difficult case, and hoped that Derik's help would prove to be invaluable. As she drove, thoughts of Mark Evans's death lingered in her mind - the mysterious disappearance of patients, the bizarre circumstances surrounding his death. Had he been involved in something sinister?

Finally, Morgan arrived at the café and parked out front. It was a quaint shop.

The café was nestled between two taller buildings, its blue and white awning stretching out over the sidewalk. The windows were adorned with green curtains and twinkling lights, the wood doors were weathered but inviting. There were a lot of memories here, and Morgan was glad to see it hadn't changed.

As if on cue, Morgan's phone buzzed in her pocket. She looked at the screen, expecting it to be Derik, but she was surprised to see it was a private number. Answering it, Morgan heard an unmistakable voice on the other end of the line.

"Special Agent Cross," a woman's voice said. A voice she'd never heard before.

And she sounded upset.

"This is me, yes," Morgan said, frowning. "Who is this?"

"He was a monster," the voice croaked. It sounded like she was crying. "I hope he rots in hell for what he did."

"Who?" Morgan's pulse raced, and she sat up, her palms growing sweaty as she realized this was no joke--this was a serious call.

But who was on the other end?

"He used us all," the voice said between sobs. "He was abusive, and he was a monster, and he deserved what he got."

Morgan's mind raced as she tried to place the voice. She had to find out more.

"I'm sorry for whatever happened to you," Morgan said gently, "but I need to know who you are talking about. Who deserved what he got? Who was the monster?"

There was a pause on the other end of the line, and Morgan could hear the woman taking deep breaths as if trying to calm herself down.

"You know who," she finally said, then hung up.

CHAPTER SEVEN

Morgan stared at Derik from across the table in the café, her hands clasped around a warm mug of black coffee. Derik stared at her, mouth agape.

"So, you have no idea where the phone call came from?"

Morgan shook her head, mind still lingering on the desperate, anonymous woman's voice. The only theory that seemed to make sense, considering the timing, was that the caller was referring to Mark Evans. Perhaps it was Eve, or maybe the woman in the waiting room.

"It could be why Mark Evans quietly lost his job," Morgan said. "The receptionist refused to elaborate, but I left my card. Maybe they quietly fired him for harassing patients and tried to cover it all up so their reputation wouldn't be ruined. They may have even paid him off to go without a fight."

Derik stroked his chin thoughtfully. "Possible, but it doesn't explain the circumstances of his death. Someone went to great lengths to pull that off. And Lisa was the first victim."

They sat in silence for a few moments, both lost in thought. Morgan's mind kept circling back to the anonymous phone call. It was untraceable now. She knew she needed to find out more about the woman who had called her. She should go back in and talk to Eve, demand to know who the woman in the waiting room was or for more of the truth. At the same time, Derik had a point; even if Mark was fired for harassment, it didn't explain why Lisa was killed first... it might not be connected to his death at all.

She made a mental note to look into it, but she didn't want to spend too much time chasing down leads without evidence.

"There's something else," Derik said, and Morgan's eyes flashed to his. "The powder in the water bottle. It was amphetamines."

Morgan's heart raced. "So, he was drugged."

"Yeah. Lisa died a week ago, and unfortunately her body has already been drained of fluids and processed for her funeral, so toxicology will be hard. But I think we can assume she was drugged too."

Morgan clenched her teeth. If they'd had this case in the first place, that was the first thing she would've demanded. But at that time, they truly didn't know if it was a murder, or just a strange case of kidnapping.

Now, they knew it was a murder. A series of them, with potentially more coming.

The evidence they did have was in that film.

"Has forensics recovered any part of the film?" Morgan asked Derik.

"They're still working on it; last I heard they had a couple potential frames, but we need someone with the expertise to try and recover it. It's old school, a real delicate process, and we don't have a specialist on our team."

Morgan took a sip of the bitter coffee, her mind swimming. There was a film school here in the city. She'd driven past it many times. "The film academy," she said. "I bet there's someone there who can help us out."

Derik's expression tightened. "Yeah... there is."

Morgan frowned. "So, what's the issue? Let's grab the evidence and head there now."

Derik sighed. "Look, there is someone I know there who could almost certainly help us, but she's sort of an ex."

Morgan could hardly believe what she was hearing. "An ex, Derik? Really?"

"Yeah, from before I got married," he said. "It's not a great situation and she's not someone I'd like to run into, so maybe you should go alone."

Morgan lifted a brow. "Derik, you've gotta be kidding me. We're professionals here."

Derik looked down, fiddling with his coffee cup. "I know, I know. It's just... complicated. I don't want things to get awkward."

Morgan sighed, feeling a twinge of annoyance. She didn't need this drama right now, but she also knew they needed that film recovered.

"Come on, Greene, let's just go."

Derik nodded, his expression pained. "Alright. But just be prepared, okay? She might not be thrilled to see me."

Morgan didn't know exactly what to expect, but she was determined to get the evidence they needed. She grabbed her coat and followed Derik out of the café.

***

Morgan saw the sprawling campus of the film academy as they pulled up to the gates. The grand entrance was illuminated by ornate lamps and the pathway leading up to the building was lined with trees.

They had gone back to HQ to retrieve the evidence, then took Derik's car together. She could feel Derik's anxiety as he drove them, but they were all adults and whenever Derik had dated this woman, it had been before he was married and then divorced, so a long time. Probably just after Morgan had gone to prison.

Morgan pushed those thoughts aside as they stepped out of the car and made their way towards the main building. Derik led the way, his eyes scanning the area as if searching for someone in particular. Morgan followed closely, feeling a mix of excitement and apprehension. They were getting closer to solving the case, but they were also walking into a potentially awkward situation.

As they entered the building, Morgan was struck by the energy and creativity of the students milling about. There were film posters plastered on the walls, equipment strewn about, and groups of people huddled together discussing their latest projects.

Derik led her down a hallway lined with classrooms until they arrived at a door labeled "Film Restoration Lab." He hesitated for a moment before knocking softly.

The door opened and a woman peered out. She had curly hair that cascaded down her shoulders, with glasses perched on the bridge of her nose. Her expression was inquisitive, as if she was studying the two visitors before her. Her skin glowed and her eyes seemed to sparkle, giving her an air of intelligence and mystery.

For a moment, Morgan didn't recognize her, but then it clicked. This was the ex that Derik had been talking about. Morgan had never seen her before.

It seemed she didn't recognize them at first either, but when her eyes fell on Derik, that inquisitive nature turned sour.

"Derik Greene?" she said, her mouth agape.

"Hey, Gloria," Derik said, rubbing the back of his neck.

"What are you doing here?" she said, glancing at Morgan.

"Work-related," Derik murmured. "This is my partner, Morgan Cross."

Morgan nodded at Gloria, who only glowered away. "I'm very busy. Can't someone else do it?"

Morgan decided to step in before this could turn hostile. "I'm afraid we're looking to restore some extremely damaged and delicate film," Morgan said. "Special Agent Greene said you're one of the best, and we need someone we can trust."

Gloria hesitated, averting her gaze.

"Please," Morgan added, "people's lives are on the line."

Derik nodded, echoing her statement. "It's important, Gloria. I wouldn't be here if it weren't."

Gloria let out a sigh, her shoulders slumping. "Fine," she said finally. "Come in."

Morgan and Derik followed her into the lab, which was cluttered with various tools and machinery. The smell of chemicals was overwhelming, and Morgan wrinkled her nose in distaste. Gloria led them to a small, dimly lit room, where a large table was set up with various equipment.

"This is where we do the actual restoration work," Gloria explained, gesturing to the table. "What do you need help with?"

Morgan pulled out an evidence bag from her pocket, filled with clippings of the film. "This," she said simply.

Gloria picked up the bag and examined it closely. "This is in pretty bad shape," she observed, her eyes scanning the exterior for any damage. "But I might be able to restore a few still frames."

Morgan breathed a sigh of relief. "That's all we need for now. Thank you, Gloria."

Gloria grimaced. "Don't thank me yet. This is going to take a while."

As Gloria set to work, Derik hovered awkwardly next to Morgan. Morgan could feel his discomfort radiating off of him in waves. She decided to break the silence.

"So, Gloria," Morgan said, "how did you get into film restoration?"

Gloria looked up, surprised at the sudden conversation. "Oh, um, it's kind of a long story. I've always been interested in film, and I stumbled upon a job opening here at the academy when I was looking for work."

Morgan nodded, intrigued. "Do you enjoy it?"

Gloria paused, her eyes distant. "It's... complicated. I love the actual work of restoring the films, but the politics and drama of working in the industry can be exhausting."

Morgan could relate to that sentiment. "I can imagine. It must be difficult to balance the creative side with the business side."

Gloria nodded, her expression solemn. "It is. Sometimes I feel like I'm drowning in it all."

Morgan wondered what had happened with Derik and Gloria, why he'd been so nervous to see her. She didn't seem thrilled by him, but she wasn't completely hostile either.

Gloria began to rummage through the various tools and equipment, selecting certain items and setting them aside. She began the process of restoring individual frames so they could be blown up in the projector she already had set up. Morgan and Derik watched in silence as Gloria began to work her magic. Her hands moved deftly over the tools, her focus intense as she examined the film clippings before beginning the restoration process.

Morgan watched intently as Gloria worked. She was impressed by her skill and attention to detail. The way she delicately handled the film, as if it were a precious artifact, was a sight to behold.

While Gloria worked, Morgan couldn't help but ponder the situation between Derik and Gloria. Was it possible that they still had feelings for each other? Or was it just the awkwardness of seeing an ex after so long? Morgan couldn't quite put her finger on it.

As Gloria continued to work, Morgan stepped back and leaned against the wall. She watched as Gloria's hands flew over the equipment, the sound of the machines whirring and humming in the background. The air was thick with tension and Morgan could tell that Derik was feeling it too.

After what felt like an eternity, Gloria finally said, "Let's test these out."

Gloria went and shut off the lights. For a moment, the room was bathed in darkness. Gloria slotted a wheel into the projector and turned it on. The machine clicked to life, filling the room with more light. Morgan watched as images took over the screen.

They were still damaged, but Morgan could see the image of a lion, snarling with bloody teeth. The next frame showed a strange black symbol over a white background.

"This is like what I saw before the film combusted," Morgan said to Gloria.

Another image, insects eating away at carrion.

Morgan heard movement beside her and looked to see Derik checking his phone. He slipped out of the room, leaving Morgan and Gloria alone. It seemed he got a phone call, and Morgan assumed it was important. She focused on the film; one more frame, highly damaged, showed a woman.

Morgan frowned. "Hold it there."

Gloria paused the projector.

Morgan stepped up to the screen. The woman's face was bubbling because of the damage, and her features were nearly indistinguishable. But Morgan thought she could make out blonde hair.

"I need to know who this is," she said aloud.

"That's the last frame," Gloria said. "I'm sorry, this was the best I could do. I can keep trying, if you'd like."

"Please do," Morgan said. "Can you turn these into digital copies and send them to us?"

"Of course." Gloria bit her lip, her eyes lingering on the image. Morgan got the sense she had more to say.

"Is something wrong?" Morgan asked.

"It's just... these frames. It reminds me of the work of someone I know."

Morgan stood up straight, crossing her arms. "Who?"

Gloria's eyes hesitantly flashed to Morgan. "Well, he used to be a director here," she said. "A long time ago. He made strange films like this, with disturbing animal imagery and sometimes strange symbols. He ended up getting fired, as the board thought his films were too disturbing for school. I haven't seen anything like this since."

Morgan's mind raced. "When did he get fired?"

"About seven years ago. I have no idea what happened to him after that."

If this were true, then maybe this man, this director, was having an artistic resurgence. Morgan needed to know more.

"Who was he? What was his name?"

Gloria hesitated for a moment, her eyes flickering with uncertainty. Morgan could sense that she was nervous about sharing this information. Eventually, Gloria took a deep breath and spoke with a tremble in her voice.

"His name was David Reed."

Morgan's eyes widened in surprise. David Reed was a name that she had heard before. He was a notorious local director in town, known for his bold and often disturbing films. Sometimes Salvador Dali-esque. But Morgan wasn't sure if he was still active. Anything she'd heard about him was from ten years ago, before she went to prison.

"Do you know where he is now?" Morgan asked, her voice low.

Gloria shook her head. "I'm sorry, I have no idea. After he was fired, he disappeared from the industry altogether. Nobody has heard from him since."

Morgan frowned. If David Reed was behind this film, then she needed to find him and figure out what he was up to.

"Thank you, Gloria," Morgan said. "You've been a huge help."

Just then, Derik burst back into the room, his face urgent. "Cross, we've gotta go."

Morgan's breath caught. "What is it?"

"It's Aaron Matthews," he said. "They found him."

CHAPTER EIGHT

Morgan took in the sight of the shaking, timid man in front of her in the interrogation room at the local police station. Aaron Matthews was exactly as she'd expected him to be based on what she'd seen in his messy room: scrawny, with unkempt hair, and a nervous energy that seemed to vibrate off of him. He fidgeted in his chair, avoiding Morgan's gaze as she sat across from him, Derik quietly observing at her side.

"Mr. Matthews," Morgan said in a calm tone, "you're a hard man to find."

Aaron scratched the back of his head. "I--I checked myself into rehab," he stammered. "I didn't know anyone was looking for me. I already told the police everything I know, so what gives?"

Morgan leaned forward, eyes firm on Aaron, even though he did everything he could to avoid her gaze. "The film you found in the warehouse," she said. "Did you destroy it before the police arrived?"

"What? No! I told that detective, it was already all burned up when I got there. I wouldn't destroy something like that."

Morgan studied Aaron's face, searching for any signs of deception. It was hard to tell with his eyes darting around the room like a trapped animal. But something about his answer didn't sit right with her.

"Can you tell us anything about the film?" she pressed. "Anything you remember about it?"

"I barely even looked at it," Aaron said, his voice shaky. "Honestly, I was a little too focused on the dead woman--" Aaron pinched his eyes shut and started rocking. "Oh God, the dead woman..."

Morgan exchanged a look with Derik. Either Aaron was genuinely traumatized by what he'd seen, or this was an act.

"We're sorry you had to witness that," Derik said. "It must've been hard."

"Yeah, well, it's not every day you walk into a warehouse and find a woman tied up to a chair, dead like that," he stammered. "Do you guys have any idea who did it?"

"No, but there's been another victim," Morgan said, checking for Aaron's reaction.

His eyes only widened. "O-oh, damn, that's not good."

"No," Morgan said. "Your roommate, Stacy, mentioned that you're prone to showing aggression during protests with your activist group. Is that true?"

Aaron shifted uncomfortably in his chair, looking down at his hands. "I mean, we're just fighting for what's right, you know? But sometimes things can get heated."

"And have you ever taken things too far?" Morgan asked.

Aaron looked back up at her, his eyes locking with hers for the first time since the interrogation began. "No," he said firmly. "I've never hurt anyone, and I never would. We're just out there to make a statement, you know?"

"Of course," Morgan said, nodding. "But sometimes things can get out of hand."

Aaron shifted in his seat, his eyes flicking back and forth between Morgan and Derik. "I mean... I'm passionate about what we're fighting for. Sometimes things get heated."

Morgan leaned in closer. "What are you fighting for, Aaron? What's so important to you that you're willing to get violent?"

"We're fighting against the corrupt corporate system," Aaron said, his voice raising in pitch. "They're destroying the environment, exploiting workers, and ruining lives. We have to do something about it."

"And what were you doing at the warehouse when you found the body?"

Aaron squirmed in his seat. "I was just... I was going to get the warehouse ready for our rally that day."

"And what did you find?" Morgan asked, her voice low and intense.

Aaron swallowed hard. "I found the film. And I found the woman. And I called the police. That's it. I didn't do anything wrong. I already told you everything I know."

Morgan sat back in her chair, studying Aaron's face. There was something about his demeanor that set her on edge, that made her think he was hiding something. But she couldn't quite put her finger on what it was.

She wasn't sure what to make of Aaron. On one hand, he was clearly a sketchy individual, but she somehow doubted he was capable of all this.

But she had the sketchbook she'd found in his room, the one with the strange symbols. She reached under the table and pulled it out, slapping it on the table.

Aaron's eyes widened. "M-my sketchbook!"

"Yes," Morgan said, flipping it open. "I noticed some strange imagery you drew in here." She opened it to an image of a knot with a cross on it. This was probably most like the image in the film, although it still wasn't a perfect match. "Why did you draw this?" Morgan asked.

"I dunno, I just doodle sometimes," Aaron said. "It doesn't really mean anything."

Morgan wasn't convinced. She turned the page and showed Aaron another image, this one more elaborate: a twisted, almost organic-looking mass with what looked like a human form at its center.

"What's this?" Morgan asked.

Aaron's eyes darted back and forth before he spoke. "It's just... something I came up with. It's not real."

"Are you sure?" Morgan asked. "It seems very deliberate."

Aaron shifted in his seat. "I-I don't know, okay? I just drew it because it looked cool. I didn't even remember drawing it until you showed me the book just now."

Morgan took out another image from her pile of evidence. A blown-up image of the symbol from the film. She inched it toward Aaron, checking his expression for his reaction, but he only looked more confused.

"Have you seen this before?" Morgan asked.

"I don't think so," Aaron said. "I didn't draw it."

It was a strange symbol, black over a white background. Morgan had never seen it before, and on the drive down to talk to Aaron from the film academy, she'd done a reverse image search that had yielded no exact match. Whatever it was, it was clearly something only the killer understood.

And maybe Aaron was just lying to save his own skin.

Morgan leaned forward, her voice low and intense. "Listen, Aaron," she said. "We've been investigating this case for a while now, and we know there's something bigger going on here. Something that involves this symbol. And if you're lying to us, we will find out. We will find out everything."

Aaron paled, and Morgan could see the fear in his eyes. But she also saw something else-- a flicker of recognition, maybe. Almost like he knew more than he was letting on.

"I-I swear to God, I don't know anything else," he said, his voice trembling. "Please, I just want to go home. I need my medication."

Morgan sat back, studying Aaron's face for a long moment. She had a feeling he wasn't telling her everything, but there was no way to prove it without more evidence.

"And I want a lawyer," Aaron cut in. "I know my rights. I want a lawyer. Or you can just let me go so I can go home and take my medication."

Morgan and Derik exchanged a glance. The request for a lawyer was a smart move on Aaron's part, but it also meant that they couldn't push him any further without incriminating themselves.

On one hand, Morgan wanted to keep him locked up. On the other, if Aaron was guilty, then if they let him go, they could use the chance to tail him and see where he was going.

"Okay," Morgan said, standing up. "You're free to go, Aaron. But please stay in town."

Aaron nodded, looking relieved. "Thank you, thank you so much," he said, standing up to leave.

As soon as he was gone, Morgan turned to Derik with a grim expression.

"There's something off about him," she said. "I don't think he's telling us everything. Let's tail him."

Derik's expression tightened. "What, right now?"

"Yeah," Morgan said. The more she vocalized it, the surer of herself she was. She stood, ready to get out there right now.

Derik stood too. "Cross, we have nothing on him. He asked for a lawyer, but we let him go. We could still get in hot water if we keep on him."

"It doesn't matter," Morgan said. "I only said he could go so we could go after him."

"This is not by the books, Cross," Derik warned.

"I know," Morgan said, grabbing her coat. "But if he's the killer, we need to catch him before he strikes again."

Derik sighed but followed her out of the interrogation room, onto the street.

It was later in the day now, overcast. Up ahead, they spotted Aaron walking down the street, and Morgan gestured for Derik to hang back as they discreetly followed him. Derik gave Morgan a disapproving look, but it didn't matter. Aaron never called a cab or got into a car, so it looked like they were following him on foot.

***

They trailed him for several blocks, watching as he walked through the downtown area and into a residential neighborhood. Morgan kept her eyes on Aaron the whole time, her suspicion of him only growing as his movements became more erratic.

"This is insane, Cross," Derik muttered as they walked. "Where do you think he's leading us? He's probably walking home."

"I know," Morgan said, determination in her voice. "But we have to find out what he knows. We have to find out what this symbol means. And if Aaron is involved, we have to bring him to justice."

Derik sighed, but he nodded in agreement.

As they rounded a corner, they saw Aaron disappear into an old, rundown factory building covered in graffiti, likely abandoned, like the warehouse Lisa had been found in. Morgan had a hunch that this was where he was heading, and she motioned for Derik to follow her as they made their way inside.

The inside of the factory was dimly lit, and the air was thick with the smell of rust and decay, with water dripping from leaky pipes and old machinery creaking in the silence. Morgan and Derik moved slowly, cautiously, trying not to make too much noise. They could hear Aaron's footsteps echoing in the distance, but they couldn't see him yet.

Morgan couldn't help but feel a shiver run down her spine as she followed Aaron's trail through the maze of old machinery and debris. Every creak and groan of the building made her more and more uneasy.

Finally, they came to an old freight elevator, and Morgan could hear voices coming from below. She motioned for Derik to stay quiet as they crept closer, trying to make out what was being said.

"...I don't know what they want from me," Aaron's voice came, tense and panicked. "I swear I don't know anything else."

Another voice, deeper but more desperate, said, "Look, man, just let me go. I don't wanna hear about all your stupid problems, I just want you to let me go."

Morgan's heart raced as she drew her gun, nodding at Derik to do the same. This was it: they had found the killer. They crept closer, stepping carefully so as not to alert anyone to their presence.

As they turned the corner, they saw Aaron standing in front of a man who was tied to a chair, ropes around his entire body.

As soon as the man saw them, his eyes widened and he yelled, "Help! Help me! This guy's nuts!"

Aaron was petrified as his eyes snapped to Morgan and Derik.

Morgan drew her gun instantly and yelled, "Freeze! FBI!"

But Aaron dashed to the side, ducking behind a piece of equipment. Morgan dashed after him, gun drawn.

"Get him, Cross!" Derik shouted, diving forward to untie the victim.

Derik stayed behind to untie the captive.

Morgan could hear Aaron's footsteps echoing in the distance as she chased him, her heart pounding in her chest. She couldn't let him get away, not again.

She turned a corner and saw him up ahead, his back to her. Morgan's muscles burned as she chased after him, hopping over equipment.

Finally, she caught up to him, grabbing him by the collar and slamming him against the wall. Aaron let out a yelp of pain as his head hit the concrete.

An image flashed in Morgan's mind.

Darren La Roux, being shoved off her, his skull connecting with the dumpster.

Morgan froze, and on instinct, she jumped back.

She couldn't go back to prison.

It couldn't happen again.

Confusion flitted over Aaron's face, and while Morgan was in a daze, he ran off. Morgan shook her head, trying to shake off the memory. She had to focus on catching the killer. She dashed after Aaron, her gun still drawn, her heart pounding with adrenaline. Morgan rushed towards the door, her heart in her throat. She burst through the door, her gun pointing straight at Aaron.

But it was too late. Aaron was nowhere to be seen.

"Shit!" Morgan yelled.

"Cross, what the hell?" Derik shouted, and Morgan turned to see him inside the building, coming toward her with the victim, the man, behind him.

Morgan scowled and turned away, her mind too cloudy to deal with Derik right now.

She'd frozen up.

She'd let the suspect get away.

And the memory of Darren was still lingering, taking over her.

"Cross!" Derik shouted.

Morgan turned to see Derik's face twisted in anger.

"I saw the whole thing," he scolded. "You pushed him away from you. You let him go. What the hell happened?"

Morgan couldn't explain it. She felt anger and confusion settling over her like smoke. "Just back off, Greene," she spat.

"What is wrong with you?" Derik asked.

"Just--leave me alone!" Morgan yelled. She pushed past Derik and stormed out of the building, feeling the cold air hit her face as she stepped outside. She leaned against the wall, feeling lightheaded and overwhelmed. She couldn't shake the memory of Darren, the way he had hit his head and lay there, lifeless.

Derik followed her out, but Morgan waved him off. "I need a minute," she said, her voice strained.

Derik hesitated, but he nodded and went back inside, leaving Morgan alone on the street.

Morgan took a deep breath, trying to calm herself down. She knew she had to keep pushing forward, had to find the killer before it was too late. But fear and doubt were creeping in, making it hard to focus. She closed her eyes, trying to will herself to be stronger, more resilient. She couldn't let her past mistakes define her future. She had to keep fighting, no matter the cost.

But because of her personal demons, she'd just let a suspect get away.

She wasn't sure how to keep fighting when everything was falling apart.

CHAPTER NINE

Damien's eyes popped open to a screen in front of his face. He was in his living room, looking at a wall with a projector screen in front of his face.

Images strobed--animals hunting. Insects feasting.

Symbols.

Then, a girl.

A smiling girl.

Oh, no...

Damien knew who she was.

But what he didn't know was what was happening to him. Or why.

His hands were bound to a chair, and he couldn't move his head. Pain settled into his eyelids as he realized that they were being forced open by something.

And those damn images kept playing.

His palms were sweaty. His heart was racing fast, his mind fully alert now that he'd regained consciousness. He didn't feel right.

All of it felt like a dream.

"H-help," he managed to say, trying to squirm away from the imagery.

The girl on the screen suddenly stopped smiling, and her face contorted into an expression of confusion. Damien tried to look away, but his eyes were still fixated on her. He felt like he was drowning in her image, unable to break free.

A voice boomed through the room, causing Damien to jump in his chair. "Welcome back, Damien," the voice said. "I see that my little experiment is working as intended."

"What experiment?" Damien managed to choke out. His throat was dry, and he felt like he had been screaming for hours.

The voice chuckled. "You're not ready for that information yet, Damien. But trust me, you will be soon enough."

Damien's mind raced as he tried to figure out what was happening to him. Had he been kidnapped? No, he was still in his own house, so it was more of a hostage situation, it seemed.

The images on the screen suddenly changed, and Damien gasped as he saw himself. It was a live feed of him, right now, in this chair. He was disheveled, scared, and completely at the mercy of whoever was controlling this experiment.

The girl on the screen reappeared, and this time, she looked horrified. Damien watched in horror as her face contorted into a scream.

It was that little girl.

Amy...

Why?

Why was he seeing this now?

The room was dark, except for the screen in front of him. It flickered with more images, and Damien gritted his teeth. He had to get out of here.

He tried to focus, looking around for any clues as to who had done this. The air was thick, making it hard to breathe. Sweat was pouring down his face, and he felt a headache coming on.

Suddenly, Damien heard a quiet creaking sound, and he turned his head towards the noise. He saw a shadowy figure standing in the corner, watching him. Damien couldn't make out any details, but he knew that, whoever it was, they were the ones behind this madness.

"You're probably wondering why you're here," the voice boomed again, causing Damien to flinch.

"Please," he said, "I'll give you whatever you want. What is it you're after? Money? I have money. Go on, take all my money, just let me go."

The shadowy figure stepped forward, but Damien couldn't turn his head to get a full look.

"It's not money I'm after, Damien," the man said, his voice cold and calculated. "Money won't give Amy Jacobs her life back."

Damien's heart sank as he realized what this must have been about. "I-I didn't mean for that to happen to her, I swear."

"You just had to take a vacation, didn't you?" the man said. "You just had to let her die."

"No!" Damien tried to pinch his eyes shut, but he couldn't. He could only look at the images as they were forced in his face.

This had to be a nightmare.

He had to wake up soon.

Damien felt a chill run down his spine as the images on the screen changed again. Another symbol, more images of animals hunting, more blood, more insects, more pictures of Amy. They became faster and faster, and Damien's heart kept racing, pounding so loud he could feel it like a drum in his skull.

The voice continued to taunt him. "You didn't have to be here, Damien. You could have saved her. But you didn't. And now, you're going to pay."

Damien struggled against his restraints, trying to free himself. But it was no use. He was trapped, at the mercy of this madman who wanted him to suffer.

And suffer, he did.

His pulse increased.

His chest tightened with pain.

And at that moment, he was sure he was going to die.

All he could do was scream, but no one was coming to save him.

CHAPTER TEN

Morgan tried to pull herself together as she and Derik sat with the victim in the precinct. The man who'd been held by Aaron in the factory was Frank Gregor, a local politician who had been taken hostage by Aaron days before. Morgan tried to focus on Frank's story, but it was hard when she could feel Derik's tension beside her, still clearly thinking about how she'd let Aaron get away.

She was still thinking about it too.

Morgan was ashamed, in truth, but she didn't know how to handle it.

"So, he just took me and tied me up and said I was gonna pay for my policy on garbage or something like that," Frank said.

"He didn't try to drug you or anything?" Derik asked. "Or show you any strange films?"

"Films? No. And there were definitely no drugs." Frank chuckled and rested his hands on his stomach. "Would've been a lot more fun if there had been."

Frank gave off a sleazy vibe, with his slicked brown hair and flippant attitude. It struck Morgan as odd that Aaron would take him, and not drug him or show him films the way the others had been. Plus, the way Frank had been tied to the chair was different from the other victims.

But that didn't mean Aaron was innocent.

He had clearly kidnapped a man, and right now, he was the most likely suspect in the murders too.

Morgan's mind wandered, thinking about Aaron and how he had gotten away. She couldn't believe that she had let him slip through her fingers.

She needed to find him, to make things right.

"Frank, can you tell us anything else about your time with Aaron?" Morgan asked, trying to bring her focus back to the present.

Frank shrugged. "No, not really. He just ranted and raved about politics and how the system was corrupt. You know, the usual stuff."

Morgan nodded, trying to hide her disappointment in the lack of information. She had hoped Frank would have something more substantial to offer.

Derik leaned forward. "Did he say anything about any films? Did you ever see anything like that with him or hear him say anything about it?"

"No," Frank said, "I don't know why you two are so stuck on this film angle. There was nothing like that. It was all politics. The guy's some nutjob activist and is mad at me because I don't think recycling is as important as, I don't know, people paying less taxes."

It was a shift in MO, that was for sure. The killer had drugged each victim and they'd died shortly after that, but Aaron had kept Frank for days.

Something felt very off here.

Just then, Morgan's phone rang.

It was Director Mueller.

She nodded at Derik, excusing herself as she slipped out of the interrogation room and into the hallway. She'd been with Derik the whole time, so she knew he hadn't had a chance to tell AD Mueller about Morgan's slip-up yet.

She hoped he never would, but she wasn't so sure.

Whatever bond Morgan and Derik had been forming before seemed to have faded, and now all she felt between them was tension.

Pushing that aside, she answered the phone. "This is Special Agent Cross."

"Cross," Mueller's stern voice said.

Morgan's stomach sank. "What's going on?"

Mueller let out a sigh. "They found another body."

****

Morgan's pulse was in her throat.

As she hurried up to the crime scene with Derik right behind her, she found herself face-to-face with yet another upper-class home. A large driveway had a fancy car parked out front, and the expensive landscaping featured trimmed shrubbery and topiaries. The exterior of the house was painted a light beige color with dark accents around the windows and doors. The windows all had elaborate frames, suggesting that the home was recently remodeled.

It added to the sense of unease, such a nice and normal home, swarmed by police officers and FBI personnel. Morgan felt like she was back at Mark Evans's house, only this one was even grander in scale.

They hurried inside, and Morgan was afraid of what they'd see.

The inside of the house was just as impressive as the outside. A grand staircase led up to the second floor, and chandeliers hung from the ceiling, casting a dim glow throughout the entryway. The air was thick with the smell of death, and Morgan could feel her stomach churning.

The body was in the living room, which was decorated with expensive furniture, plush carpets, and ornate paintings on the walls. Morgan felt a pang of sadness thinking about how this beautiful home was now the site of yet another murder.

She pushed past the line of officers to the living room, where the scene explained itself.

Tied up to a chair, the same way the other victims had been, was a man, likely in his fifties. Although daylight seeped into the room, there was a projector set up playing a film against the wall.

Morgan's throat tightened. She couldn't believe it.

They finally had a chance to see a film, undamaged.

"Don't touch the projector," Morgan warned the room, and the personnel nodded quietly as they all watched the scene unfold.

Images of animals hunting.

Blood and carnage.

Insects feasting.

Symbols...

Then a little girl.

A child.

Smiling.

Then frowning.

Morgan's stomach twisted. Who was this girl?

She recalled the footage they'd managed to recover from Mark Evans's site. The woman, although obscured, appeared to be an adult with blonde hair. This was a tiny brunette girl, no older than eight.

Morgan took out her phone and began recording the film. The last time they had tried to touch the projector, it had combusted, and Morgan was certain the same thing would happen again this time.

But they could still record it all.

As the film continued playing, Morgan couldn't help but feel a sense of unease. The images were gruesome and unsettling, and the little girl's appearance only added to the feeling of dread. Who was she, and what did she have to do with these murders?

Morgan knew that they needed to find out more about this girl. She turned to Derik, who was standing beside her, his face twisted in disgust.

"We need to find out who this girl is," she said to him.

"I agree," Derik said. "But how do we even begin? There's not much to go on here."

Morgan nodded. He was right. They didn't have much to go on, but they couldn't afford to give up now. They needed to find out who this girl was and what her connection was to the murders.

As the footage played on, the room grew eerily quiet, save for the sounds of the film projector clicking away. The images on the wall were disturbing, grotesque even, and Morgan could feel her skin crawl with every passing second. She wondered how someone could make something so vile, so cruel.

Derik stood next to her, taking it all in. She could tell that he was just as disturbed as she was. They were partners, but they were also human. No one could watch this kind of footage and not feel something.

The film ended abruptly, and the room was plunged into darkness. Morgan snapped off her phone and slipped it back into her pocket. The officers started moving around again, snapping photos, and collecting evidence.

Morgan leaned closer to the victim, studying him. He was older than the others, and his hair was thinning. He wore a gold wedding band on his finger, and his shirt was wrinkled. There was a small cut above his eyebrow, and his skin was pale.

She wondered who he was, and what his story was. She wondered if he had a family, and if they were going to come home to find him like this.

Morgan saw there were photos on the walls of the man with an older woman and another younger woman, likely his daughter: on a beach, in front of monuments. They looked like a happy family who traveled often.

She turned to one of the officers on the scene and asked, "Do we know who he is?"

The man nodded. "Damien Ferguson. He's a general surgeon at the hospital here. His wife and daughter are away visiting family in another town."

"So, he was home alone," Morgan said. "And the girl on the video. Do we know who she is?"

The officer only shrugged.

Of course.

They'd have to do some digging, to try and match the girl with someone's identity.

Morgan felt a sense of urgency wash over her. They needed to find out who this little girl was and fast. The killer was getting bolder, and the murders were becoming more gruesome with each passing day. They couldn't afford to let another victim fall prey to the killer's twisted game.

Morgan turned to Derik, her eyes locking onto his. "We need to find out who this girl is, and we need to do it fast."

Derik nodded, his gaze just as intense as hers. "Agreed. I'll get the tech team on it right away."

Morgan's mind raced with possibilities. Who was this girl, and why was she in the footage? Was she a witness, a victim, or something else entirely?

Morgan left the living room and went outside, breathing in the fresh air as she tried to clear her head. She looked around the front yard, taking in the pristine landscaping and the expensive car parked in the driveway. It was all so normal, so perfect, and yet there was a dead man inside and a little girl in the video that she needed to identify. It was entirely possible that Aaron had pulled this off, as they didn't yet know how long Damien had been dead.

And Morgan had him.

Right in her grasp, she'd had Aaron, and the memory of Darren La Roux had caused her to choke up.

It was like Darren was still alive, punishing her, even after he was dead.

Morgan's phone rang. She answered it, expecting to hear from one of her team members, but instead heard a familiar voice.

"Morgan? It's Gloria," came the voice on the other end. "I think you should come back down to the academy--I've recovered a few more frames that I think you need to see."

CHAPTER ELEVEN

Morgan rushed into the film academy for the second time that day, this time, without Derik.

Gloria was already waiting for Morgan back at the lab. Morgan rushed in to see her standing by with the film spread out in front of her. She looked up when Morgan arrived.

"Special Agent Cross, you're here!" Gloria exclaimed.

"What do you have?" Morgan asked, her heart racing.

"I managed to enhance a few more frames from the video, and I printed them off as stills," she said, handing the photos over to Morgan. "Take a look."

Morgan scanned through the photos, her heart racing as she saw a woman's face. The blonde woman, who had soulful eyes. There was something about her that tugged at her heartstrings, something that made her want to protect her.

But there was something familiar too.

Morgan had seen this woman before. She was sure of it.

But where?

Morgan looked up at Gloria. The woman truly had no idea how helpful this was. "Thank you," Morgan said. "Seriously. This is huge. This case is getting deeper and--" Morgan stopped herself, because Gloria wasn't even a friend, let alone her therapist. "Just, thank you," Morgan said, recovering.

Plus, it was nice to be in the presence of another woman, not Derik or AD Mueller, or anyone else. She'd been around only women for ten years, and apparently, she'd gotten used to their company.

"You're welcome," Gloria said. She paused, glancing behind Morgan. "Is Derik not here?"

"He's not," Morgan said, "he's running down other leads at the moment, so I came alone."

"Good..." Gloria trailed off, but Morgan could tell she wanted to add more.

Morgan couldn't resist the pull of curiosity: "What happened between you two, anyway?"

63

Gloria hesitated for a moment, her eyes momentarily flickering with emotion. "It's complicated," she said finally, her voice low. "We were together for a while, but it just didn't work out. We both wanted different things."

Morgan nodded, sensing that there was more to the story than that.

"It's been a long time since then," Gloria added on, "but to be honest with you, Morgan, no one has ever hurt me the way Derik Greene did."

Morgan's heart sank as Gloria spoke. She wasn't good with emotions, but she knew heartbreak when she saw it. Gloria was still hurting, and it was clear that the pain was still fresh in her mind.

Still, it surprised Morgan.

"I never knew Derik as much of a heartbreaker," Morgan said. "Mind if I ask what he did?"

Gloria hesitated for a moment before sighing. "It's not really what he did, it's more about what he didn't do. He can be heartless, Morgan. I'm surprised you don't know that."

Morgan had known Derik Greene for a long time, and "heartless" was never something she knew him as.

She thought back to the other night, when she'd come over to his house, drunk, and kissed him.

How he'd pushed her away.

He hadn't exactly been cold, just firm in his rejection. Then, just last night, he'd told her he did have feelings for her, but wanted to keep things professional. Maybe it all boiled back down to what he'd said before—about not believing in love anymore, at least not for himself. Maybe he didn't want to get close to Morgan because he was scared of feeling again, of trusting. She could understand that.

She wondered what he'd done to Gloria but was afraid to press for more. For one, it wasn't her business, and two, she didn't really want to know the answer.

"Sorry about all that," Morgan said.

Gloria nodded with a tight-lipped smile. "Just be careful."

Morgan frowned. "Be careful? He's my partner, Gloria. I might not know him as a boyfriend like you did, but I know I can rely on him on the field."

"But you're not just partners, are you?" Gloria asked boldly.

Morgan's eyebrows shot up in surprise. "What do you mean?" she asked, her voice a little higher than usual.

"I mean, there's something there, isn't there? Something between you two?" Gloria said, her eyes locking onto Morgan's.

Morgan's heart rate increased as she felt a flush rising to her cheeks. She wasn't used to discussing her personal life with others, especially not someone like Gloria who she barely knew. "I don't know what you're talking about," she said.

Gloria chuckled, shaking her head. "Please, Morgan. I'm not blind. I can see the way you two look at each other, the way you touch each other. It's obvious."

Morgan's mind raced as she tried to come up with a response. She didn't want to deny it, but she didn't want to confirm it either. "It's complicated," she finally said, echoing Gloria's earlier words.

"I understand," Gloria said, her tone softening. "Believe me, I do. But just be careful."

Morgan nodded, her mind still reeling from the conversation. She knew Gloria was right. There was something between her and Derik, something that she couldn't deny anymore. But she didn't know what to do about it. She couldn't just act on her feelings, not when they were partners and had a case to solve.

She needed to focus on the case, to put her feelings aside for the time being. She looked back down at the stills, studying the woman's face once again. There was something about her that nagged at Morgan, something that she couldn't quite put her finger on. She needed to find out who this woman was, to figure out her connection to Damien and the little girl in the video and everything else.

Morgan took a deep breath, trying to clear her head. "Thank you again, Gloria. I need to get back to the office and go over these stills with the team."

"Of course," Gloria said, handing the stills back to Morgan. "Let me know if you need anything else."

Morgan nodded, then headed out of the lab. As she walked down the hallway, she couldn't help but think about Derik again. She couldn't deny her feelings for him, but she had to admit, the conversation with Gloria had left her feeling sour.

As she left the school, stepping outside, the sun was beginning to sink lower in the sky. It was getting later in the day, and the killer's timeline was escalating fast.

She headed back to her car, getting inside, just as a memory hit her.

The place she'd seen the woman before.

It was earlier today...
At Mark Evans's office.
The woman in the waiting room.

***

Morgan stormed into the office Mark Evans had worked in just before it was closing. Eve, the receptionist, was milling about, tidying up, when Morgan stormed in. Eve looked up at Morgan in shock, certainly not happy to see her there again.

"I-it's you," Eve stammered.

Morgan didn't have time to mess around. "The woman in the waiting room earlier," Morgan said. "Who was she?"

Eve's eyebrows shot up. "I'm sorry, you know I can't tell you that."

Morgan held up one of the photos from Gloria, and Eve frowned.

"What is this?" Eve asked.

"This was on a film playing in Mark Evans's house at the time he died," Morgan said. "This is no game, Eve. I know you have a job to do, but I don't have time to do this by the books. We can get all the necessary warrants we need, or you can just tell me who the woman is. I'm certain she called me after I left earlier."

Eve bit her lip, turning away. Her cheeks were scarlet red. "She didn't call you, Agent Cross... I did."

Morgan frowned, taken aback. She hadn't recognized her voice on the phone, but she'd been very shaky and distraught. "You? Why? Were you talking about Mark on the phone?"

Eve hugged herself, glancing around the empty office. Then, she sighed in defeat. "Come into one of the offices. I'm the only one left. I'll tell you everything I know."

Morgan followed Eve to one of the empty offices and sat down, ready to hear what the receptionist had to say.

"I didn't want to tell you earlier, but..." Eve trailed off, taking a deep breath. "Mark was seeing that woman, the one in the photo. Her name is Lila. She was a patient of his before he was let go."

Morgan blinked in surprise. "Lila? Do you know her last name?"

"You will have to get a warrant for that," Eve said. "I am not losing my job because of a bastard like Mark Evans."

Morgan nodded. That was fine. She had a first name, and she could find out Lila's true identity based on that.

What was more important to her was why Mark was such a bad guy.

"Okay, why was Mark really let go? What happened?"

Eve bit her lip. "He... he exploited his female patients," she said. "And he exploited me too."

Morgan leaned forward, her eyes wide with shock. "Exploited? How?"

Eve hesitated for a moment before speaking. "He would make inappropriate advances towards me, tell me things he shouldn't have. And he would do the same to his patients. He would take advantage of them in their vulnerable state, use his position of power to manipulate them."

Morgan clenched her fists, feeling a surge of anger towards Mark Evans. "Did you report him?"

Eve shook her head. "I was too scared. He was my boss, and I needed the job. And I didn't think anyone would believe me."

Morgan rested a hand on Eve's shoulder, offering her a small smile. "I believe you," she said. "So that's why you called me and called him a monster."

"I was very upset to hear he had died," Eve said. "I didn't want it to go down this way. The owner of the practice, Dr. Carmichael, wanted to keep everything quiet once he found out what was going on, but I felt so dirty for not reporting him. And now he's dead."

Morgan could see the guilt etched on Eve's face, and she felt a pang of sympathy for the young receptionist. She had been put in a difficult position, and Mark Evans had taken advantage of her vulnerability.

But Morgan had to push those feelings aside. She needed to focus on the case, on finding out who this Lila woman was and what her connection to Damien and the little girl in the video was.

"Eve, did Mark ever mention anything about a little girl?" Morgan asked.

Eve shook her head. "No, I don't think so. But he did have a lot of patients. It's possible he could have mentioned her to someone else."

Morgan nodded. "Okay. Thank you for your help, Eve. I'll make sure to keep your name out of it as much as possible."

Eve nodded, looking relieved. "Thank you, Agent Cross. I appreciate it."

Morgan got up from her seat, tucking the stills and her phone into her pocket. "I'll be in touch," she said before leaving the office.

Outside, the sky was turning pink and orange as the sun set over the city. Morgan took a deep breath, trying to clear her head. She had a lot of leads to follow up on, but she was determined to solve this thing.

She got into her car and went on her laptop, looking in the database for women named Lila who were registered to Mark's practice. It wasn't the most common name, and there was only one woman named Lila on the list.

Lila Bennett.

Morgan looked her up and found that her ID photo was an exact match to the woman seen on the film.

Lila was twenty-seven and active on social media. Morgan went to her social media page and did a quick scroll, only to see that the images--the ones Gloria had been able to recover--were matched to public videos of Lila.

Morgan pressed play on one and felt an eerie sensation run down her spine.

This was one of the videos used in the film.

Whoever had put the film together had taken it straight from Lila's social media. But how did that person know Lila was a victim?

And how, if at all, did Lila connect to Lisa or Damien, the other two victims?

None of it made sense, but Morgan needed Lila to come in and talk immediately.

Just as she was about to make a phone call, her phone rang in her hand.

It was Derik.

She promptly answered, and Derik said, "Cross, get back to HQ. I have something you need to see."

CHAPTER TWELVE

"Her name is Amy Jacobs," Derik said, standing across from Morgan in the briefing room at HQ. He slapped a photo of a little girl on the table, and Morgan's stomach twisted.

This was her.

The girl from the video.

"She died," Derik said, and Morgan's stomach plummeted.

"What? How?"

"Waiting for an operation that Damien was meant to do," Derik said. "I guess she was on a waiting list, and the surgery got pushed back a week while Damien went on vacation with his family."

Morgan could hardly believe what she was hearing. So, Damien, at least in someone's eyes, hadn't been such a great person.

Neither had Mark.

Less was known about Lisa, but Morgan remembered the article she'd read about how Lisa had defended someone accused of human trafficking in court and got them a lesser sentence.

This was it, the thing that linked all three victims. None of them were necessarily good people.

"Mark Evans was accused of sexually exploiting his female patients," Morgan said. "I identified the woman on his video too. I called her in for questioning, so someone is grabbing her right now."

"Shit," Derik cursed. He leaned his palms against the table and sighed. "So, what does this all mean?"

Morgan thought on it. If this were all true, then only one theory seemed sound. She met Derik's eyes and said: "I think we have a vigilante on our hands here."

Derik's eyes widened. "A vigilante?" he repeated. "What, someone who's killing people that they think deserve it?"

Morgan nodded gravely. "From what we know so far, Damien, Lisa, and Mark all had some sort of skeletons in their closet. It's possible that someone is taking justice into their own hands."

Derik sat back in his chair, running a hand through his hair. "Jesus. So, you think it's Aaron?"

"Aaron obviously kidnapped that politician, but the MO doesn't sync with the rest of them," Morgan said, thinking out loud. "None of their crimes are related to causes Aaron seems to care about, and the manner in which he held Frank is so different from the others. I definitely think we need to keep Aaron on our radar, but there's someone else I want to talk to also."

Derik lifted a brow. "Who?"

Morgan sat down and shuffled in, leaning her elbows over the table. She thought back to David Reed, the director Gloria had mentioned.

"Gloria mentioned a director, David Reed," Morgan said. "Maybe you've heard of him."

"I'm not really into movies," Derik said. "What about him?"

"Gloria said the frames from the film reminded her of Reed's work." Morgan took out her phone and looked up David Reed, pulling up a video of his work. Derik leaned closer as Morgan pressed play, and strange imagery filled the phone screen.

First, a mime making a sad face.

Then, wasps swarming a nest.

A church.

Several different, strange images. But it wasn't quite as bloody as the videos that the victims had been watching before they died. There were some key differences, but the style certainly could match up.

"It's pretty similar," Morgan said.

"I don't know," Derik said, scratching his head. "It's possible, but we can't just jump to conclusions."

Morgan nodded, knowing he was right. They needed more evidence before they could make any accusations. This style was similar, but not an exact match.

Still, Morgan wanted to know more about this David Reed guy.

Derik watched the video intently, his expression unreadable. "It's definitely strange," he said. "But I don't know if it's enough to connect him to the murders."

"I agree," Morgan said. "But it's worth looking into, right?"

"I don't know. Why would a director randomly go on a killing spree? What's his motive?"

"Well, he was fired from the academy a few years back," Morgan explained.

"Then he'd be after people who work there, wouldn't he? Or people connected to that world?"

"Maybe," Morgan said. "But it's possible that he sees these people as deserving of punishment. Perhaps he thinks that they're corrupt or immoral and that he's doing the world a favor by taking them out."

Derik leaned back in his chair, deep in thought. "Let's look into Reed. That might convince me more."

Morgan wondered if his doubts were because the information had come from Gloria, but she hoped he wasn't that petty. As she opened her laptop, she thought back to the conversation she'd had with Gloria, about how Derik had been heartless to her. Her curiosity gnawed at her, and she was tempted to ask about it, to get Derik's side.

On one hand, it wasn't her business.

On the other, if there was even a chance that she didn't know Derik as well as she thought, she wanted to know.

"Speaking of Gloria," she said, "she mentioned something about your falling out."

"Oh, yeah?" Derik almost laughed, leaning back in his chair. "What'd she say?"

"That you're heartless," Morgan said.

Derik chuckled, shaking his head. "That woman is something else," he said. "We had a fling a while back, nothing serious. When I ended it, she didn't take it well."

Morgan raised a brow. "So, she's just bitter?"

"Seems like it," Derik said. "She's been trying to get back at me ever since. It's nothing to worry about."

Morgan nodded, but a part of her couldn't help but wonder if there was more to the story. Gloria hadn't seemed like she was lying. And she didn't seem vengeful either.

She also apparently felt that their relationship was more serious than Derik did.

That didn't make Derik a villain. There was a chance they'd just miscommunicated. Morgan wouldn't know--she wasn't there.

She was in prison.

"I see," she said. "Well, I hope you two can patch things up."

Derik shrugged. "It makes no difference to me."

For the first time, Morgan felt like she was seeing that heartless side Gloria had mentioned. Or, at least, a careless side.

Morgan turned back to her laptop, searching for any information on David Reed in the FBI database. He had no criminal record or history of mental health issues, but it seemed he hadn't worked in a long time.

In fact, after getting fired from the academy, he'd apparently left the industry altogether.

Despite all that, he was very wealthy. His strange films had made a name for themselves in the art scene across the country. What wasn't clear to Morgan was his address; he owned several properties but didn't seem to stay fixed at any of them. One of them was a mansion on the outskirts of town, which could be a good place for a recluse to retire. But officially, it was his daughter, Ellie, who lived there.

Morgan leaned back in her chair, staring at the screen. There was something off-putting about David Reed. She couldn't quite put her finger on it, but the more she read up on him, the more convinced she became that he was connected to the murders.

"What do you think?" she asked Derik, who was focused on his own laptop.

"Hmm?" Derik looked up, distracted. "About what?"

"David Reed," Morgan said. "Are you looking into him?"

"Right," Derik said. "He doesn't seem overly suspicious or connected to me. His work is strange, but still fairly different from the films."

"But we know the killer has a theatrical flair, and it's possible he's adjusted his style to fit this new 'project,' if we can call it that," Morgan said. "He obviously enjoys putting on a show, both for the police and his victims."

Derik nodded, considering her words. "You're right. We can't rule him out yet."

Derik opened his mouth to speak, just as an intern rushed into the room, an urgent look on his face. "Agents Cross and Greene--we got Aaron Matthews."

***

Once more, Morgan found herself faced off against Aaron in an interrogation room.

This time, she wouldn't let him get away.

She still cursed herself for freezing up earlier, and she thanked her saving graces for giving them another chance. They had Aaron, and if he really was the killer, this time they'd find out.

Morgan sat across from Aaron, the table between them. Derik stood in the corner of the room, watching their every move. Morgan studied

72

Aaron's face, looking for any signs of guilt or deceit. He seemed calm and collected, his expression blank, as though he'd given up. It was a different demeanor from the shaky, sketchy guy she'd talked to earlier.

"You know why you're here, Aaron?" Morgan asked, her voice steady.

Aaron shrugged, his eyes flickering to Derik. "I have a feeling," he said.

Morgan leaned forward, her gaze locked on Aaron's. "You kidnapped Frank Gregor. And we think you know more about that woman's death, and the other deaths, than you're letting on."

Aaron's eyes flashed, his face twisting into a scowl. "Yeah, I kidnapped Gregor. I wanted him to pay, to make an example out of him, to show him that activists like me aren't going to just sit there while people like him destroy our planet and society. But I had nothing to do with those other people, I swear."

Morgan didn't believe him. There was something off about Aaron, something that made her skin crawl. Maybe there was something beyond Aaron's words that convinced her he was connected to the murders.

"Why did you kill that woman?" Morgan asked, her voice low and steady.

Aaron shook his head. "I didn't. I swear."

"Then what happened to her?" Morgan pressed.

"I don't know. I don't know anything about her."

Morgan leaned back in her chair, eyeing Aaron carefully. She needed something more, some kind of evidence that could tie Aaron to the murders.

But she had to admit, the MOs didn't match, and Morgan still had that feeling about David Reed. She was itching to talk to him, but she had to rule Aaron out.

"You said you wanted to make an example out of Frank Gregor," Morgan said, her eyes narrowed. "What kind of example?"

Aaron hesitated before answering, his eyes flickering to the door. "I wanted to show him that people like us won't tolerate his greed and disregard for the environment. That we're willing to take action."

"What kind of action?" Morgan asked.

Aaron looked down at his hands, twisting his fingers. "I don't know," he said finally. "I never meant for anyone to die. I just wanted to scare him."

Morgan leaned forward again. "You're not telling us everything, Aaron. We know you have something to do with those murders."

Aaron shook his head. "I swear, I don't. I'm not a killer."

Morgan glanced back at Derik, who appeared just as exhausted as she was. This was going nowhere, and Morgan didn't want to waste any more time on Aaron.

"Alright, we're done here," Morgan said, standing up. "But don't think this is over. You have a lot to answer for, Aaron. You're not going anywhere."

Aaron stayed silent, his eyes fixed on the table.

As they left the room, Derik turned to Morgan. "You think he's telling the truth?"

Morgan shook her head. "I don't know, but something about him makes me think he's not telling us everything."

Derik nodded in agreement. "We need to keep looking into him, but we also need to start pursuing other leads."

Morgan nodded. "Agreed. And one of those leads needs to be David Reed."

Derik raised a brow. "You really think he's connected to the murders?"

"I do," Morgan said. "There's just something about him that doesn't sit right with me. Let's pay him a visit. Let me just grab something from my office." She needed a drink of water, realizing she hadn't had any fluids other than coffee all day. She'd left her bottle in her office, so went to swing by and grab it.

Morgan opened the door to her office, but stopped when she noticed something strange. Something that definitely wasn't there before.

A white envelope on her desk.

CHAPTER THIRTEEN

Morgan's hands shook as she walked toward the envelope, facing upright on her desk. She wasn't sure why, but something about it felt off--like she was about to touch an explosive device.

Obviously, one of her colleagues must have dropped it off. But she'd never known anyone in the FBI to be leaving love notes on her desk, or to not label paperwork.

A lump formed in her throat, but she swallowed it. Derik leaned into her office and said, "Hey, what's the hold up?"

Morgan turned back to him. "Did you leave this on my desk?"

Derik shook his head. "No, I'd just call if I had information. Why, what's wrong?"

Morgan took a deep breath and picked up the envelope. It was heavier than she expected. For a moment, she was paranoid that it had something to do with Darren, somehow. Her heart pounded as she slid her finger under the flap and tore it open.

Inside were several photos of a woman she'd never seen before. Pale skin, brown hair, and blue eyes, smiling at the camera like it was nothing. Selfies, group photos--like with Lila, Morgan got the sense these were pulled from the woman's social media account.

If that were the case, then like Lila, this person could be a victim of someone else's crimes.

Someone else...

Who might now be the killer's next target.

Derik appeared over Morgan's shoulder. "Who is this?"

"I don't know, but we need to find out," Morgan said. "If this is what I think it is, then this woman... might tell us who our next victim is."

Morgan quickly gathered her things, shoving the envelope into her bag. They had to move fast. As they left the office, Morgan's mind raced with questions. Who was this woman? How was she connected to the murders? And most importantly, how could they find her before it was too late for someone else?

Morgan knew they needed to act quickly, and she had a feeling that time was running out. She could feel the pressure building, and she needed to find a way to relieve it. She needed to find a way to catch the killer before it was too late.

They made their way to the tech lab, where Garcia was waiting for them. "What's up, my intrepid FBI agents?" she asked, a huge smile on her face.

"We need you to run facial recognition on these photos," Morgan said, pulling out the envelope and handing it to Garcia. "We think this woman might be associated with the next victim."

Garcia's smile faded as she looked at the photos. "Oh, my God," she said softly. "I'll get on it right away."

Morgan and Derik watched as Garcia hurriedly set up her equipment. They both knew time was of the essence, and they couldn't afford to waste any more of it.

As they waited, Morgan tried to keep her mind focused on the task at hand. She couldn't think about the fact that they were dealing with a serial killer, that people were dying because of them. She couldn't let the weight of that reality crush her.

She also wanted to know who the hell had put that envelope in her office.

There were cameras in the hallways, but Morgan knew for a fact that the camera didn't happen to hit her office. It had been a minor issue before, during her sentencing when she went to prison, when she'd tried to claim she was in her office doing paperwork at a time that couldn't be proved. Not that it would have made a difference anyway. That night, Morgan had been framed for murder, and nothing would have stopped it from happening.

Someone in the FBI had been working against her.

She knew that now.

An agent had reported her, and Morgan was painfully reminded of that fact. She glanced around the room, suddenly nervous, unsure who to trust if anyone at all.

Garcia spoke, ending Morgan's train of thought: "I have a hit," she said. "This is Bella Hunt, a college student. She was shot and killed by an officer on duty about a year ago, a complete accident during a face-off with another criminal."

Morgan's heart sank. Another victim of circumstance.

"Wait, an accidental shooting? Who was the officer?"

Garcia clicked away on her computer for a moment before turning back to Morgan. "Officer Owen Fernandez. He was released after the incident and didn't even lose his badge, since it was a confirmed accident, and he was on-duty."

Morgan's heart sank.

Owen Fernandez.

This was him.

The killer's next target.

Morgan knew they needed to act fast to catch the killer before he struck again, and this time it was Owen Fernandez, an officer who had accidentally killed Bella Hunt. The killer was targeting people who had played a role in the death of others or were victims of circumstance.

Morgan's mind raced as she tried to come up with a plan. They had to find Owen before the killer did. They couldn't afford to lose another victim.

"We need to find Owen Fernandez," Morgan said, her voice urgent. "Now."

***

It was dark by the time Morgan and Derik pulled outside of Owen's house. The single-story family home stood in the evening, its small windows glowing with warm yellow light. Morgan hopped out of the passenger seat of Derik's car, rushing up to the front door and banging hard. Derik hurried up behind her.

Morgan fidgeted anxiously as she waited for an answer. Finally, after several tense moments, a woman in her thirties answered the door, looking at them with concern. Morgan had read that Owen Fernandez had a wife, and this must be her.

"Ma'am, we're with the FBI," Morgan said, flashing her badge. "We need to speak with Owen Fernandez. It's a matter of urgency."

The woman's eyes widened with fear. "Is he in trouble? What's going on?"

Morgan didn't have time to sugar-coat things. "We believe he's in danger. We need to find him now."

The woman's face paled as she stepped back and let them inside. "He's not here," she said, her voice trembling. "I haven't seen him since last night."

Morgan's heart sank. They were too late.

"Do you have any idea where he might be?" Derik asked, taking charge of the situation.

The woman shook her head, tears streaming down her face. "No, he didn't leave a note or anything. He just said he had to go out and left."

Morgan's mind raced as she tried to come up with a plan. They had no idea where the killer could have taken Owen, and time was running out. They needed to find him before it was too late.

"We were fighting," the woman said, her voice trembling. "I thought... I thought maybe he went out with his buddies, and I wanted to give him space, so I didn't call him. You don't really think he's in danger, do you?"

Morgan exchanged a worried look with Derik. "Ma'am, we can't say for certain, but given the circumstances, it's a possibility."

The woman started to cry harder, her hands shaking as she held onto the kitchen counter. "Please, you have to find him," she said, looking at them with pleading eyes. "He's a good man; he didn't do anything wrong."

"We'll do everything we can," Morgan said firmly. "But we need your help. Is there anyone Owen might have gone to see? Any friends or family members?"

The woman shook her head. "No, he's been distant lately. I don't know who he talks to anymore."

Morgan felt a sense of frustration building inside of her. They were running out of leads, and every second that passed was one more second that Owen could be in danger.

The best bet they had was the knowledge that the killer, whoever he was, had an obsession with films. They could check every movie theater, any potentially abandoned cinemas. But considering some victims had been killed at home, the search seemed near impossible.

Either way, they had to try.

"We'll do everything we can, ma'am," Morgan said, before she turned back to the car.

They needed a gameplan, and they needed one now.

***

Morgan kicked in the door to the abandoned cinema on the outskirts of town, her gun drawn and at the ready. Her eyes scanned the dark and eerie shadows that lingered in the corners of the building. Her stance was composed and alert, her body ready to take action at a moment's notice.

Derik was right behind her, and he peered into the abandoned cinema. Morgan's eyes slowly adjusted to the darkness as she took in the area. Cobwebs hung from the ceiling, weaving between the broken and dusty shelves of the concession stand. The concrete walls were streaked with years of grime and neglect, and through it all Morgan could make out a few old posters, faded by time but still clinging to the walls.

They had every available hand in the city searching for Owen Fernandez, and this old theater was just one of many stops. She locked eyes with Derik, and they both nodded as they began their search of the building.

As they crept through the theater, Morgan couldn't shake the feeling that they were being watched. Every creak of the old wooden floorboards made her heart skip a beat. The sound of their footsteps echoed unnaturally throughout the empty theater, adding to her paranoia. She kept her gun close, ready to fire at a moment's notice.

They moved cautiously through the rows of seats, the floorboards creaking beneath their feet. Morgan's ears strained to catch any sound that might indicate Owen's presence, but all she could hear was the sound of her own breathing and her heart pounding in her chest.

They had searched almost the entirety of the abandoned cinema and had found no trace of Owen. Or the killer.

There was no movie playing.

Nothing.

She met back with Derik in the main lobby. His shoulders slumped, and he let out a long sigh.

"He's not here," he said.

"Damn it." Morgan bit her lip anxiously, then took out her phone. She called AD Mueller, and his strong voice came through on the other end.

"Cross, what is it?"

"Has anyone found anything, sir?" Morgan asked.

"You'll be the first I call when I hear about it," Mueller said. "I take it your location didn't pan out."

"No." Morgan grit her teeth. "Where the hell is this guy?"

"I don't know, but you better find out," Mueller said, then the line went dead.

Morgan turned away, frustration coursing through her. They'd lost too many victims, and she was starting to feel like a failure in more ways than one. Everything with Darren, now this case--it was all piling up on her.

"Maybe Owen isn't a target," Derik reasoned.

"Then why the hell would those pictures be on my desk?" Morgan asked. "And who put them there?"

She couldn't believe that this was all for nothing.

Owen Fernandez was out there somewhere, in danger, and they had to find him. But this theater was the last location on their list. If they weren't here, then Morgan had no idea where they were.

There had to be some place they'd missed.

Then it hit her.

The drive-in theater.

Morgan remembered when she was younger how her dad would take her there to watch movies under the stars. She remembered the old car they had bought specifically for their outdoor adventures and how they'd laugh and talk until late into the night. She recalled the smell of popcorn in the air, and the twinkle of stars above them in a blanket of pure darkness that seemed almost magical. Her heart swelled with nostalgia as she thought about all those childhood memories that were made at that drive-in theater.

But now, it could be used for something far more sinister.

"Derik," Morgan said cautiously, "I think I know where he is."

CHAPTER FOURTEEN

When they arrived at the abandoned drive-in, Morgan felt a sense of dread rush over her as she saw its familiar structure silhouetted against the night sky. The large screen still stood tall, framed by rows of broken-down speakers lined up in front of it like silent sentries watching over their kingdom. The gravel parking lot was cracked with age, but Morgan remembered how busy this place used to be when she'd come here as a kid on summer nights with her family. She could almost hear laughter from days past echoing through the silent air.

It seemed so much smaller than Morgan remembered it being, but it also filled her with nostalgia. She shook those memories off.

In the stillness of the night, there could be something far worse going on here.

Morgan gestured to Derik to follow her as they crept towards the main entrance. The door was locked tight, but Morgan had dealt with her fair share of locked doors before. She pulled out her lock picking kit and got to work.

As the door clicked open, they stepped inside, and Morgan felt a sense of unease settle in her stomach. The drive-in theater was completely abandoned, the only sound coming from the creaks of the old wooden boards beneath their feet.

"Stay alert," Morgan whispered to Derik. "We don't know what we might find in here."

They moved cautiously through the rows of empty parking spaces, their eyes scanning the darkness. The only light came from a flickering screen in the distance, casting eerie shadows across the gravel.

Something was playing on the far screen.

A film.

Every instinct in Morgan shocked to life.

This was it.

Owen was here--she was sure of it.

She motioned to Derik, and the two of them began to move more quickly, staying low to avoid being seen.

As they got closer, they could hear the faint sound of a projector flickering. Morgan slowly drew her gun, her fingers gripping it tightly as they advanced. The closer they got, the more the images became clearer.

Animals hunting.

Strange symbols.

Then, a girl...

The girl from the photos.

The girl Owen had killed.

It was being forced in his face, a form of psychological torture, to punish him for what he'd done. Morgan darted into a sprint, her muscles burning as she ran through the field toward the giant screen.

And there, sitting on a lone chair in the middle of an empty lot, was a man.

Morgan stopped, her heels skidding in the dirt. Derik appeared behind her, and she heard him let out a small breath.

They could both see it, as clear as day.

They were too late.

Morgan sprinted into action anyway, darting in front of Owen even on the small chance that he was still alive. But as she rounded to his front, it was clear that he was dead. His body was stiff and tied to the chair. His eyes were wide open, devoid of life, his mouth slack.

He'd died, the same way the others had.

Alone, tied to a chair, being forced to watch a film that reminded them of the people they'd hurt, whether they had intended to or not.

Morgan's heart sunk into her chest. She'd failed again. And this time, it was far worse than any previous failure. This was someone's life, a young man who had been brutally murdered while they were wasting time searching in the wrong place.

Derik stepped closer to the body, examining it thoroughly. Morgan couldn't bear to look at Owen's lifeless face and turned away.

"We're too late," Morgan said, her voice barely above a whisper. "Owen's dead."

Derik put a hand on her shoulder, offering support as they waited for the other officers to arrive. Morgan felt numb, the weight of failure heavy on her shoulders. She couldn't help but wonder how many more victims would fall prey to this killer before they were caught.

"We'll get him," Derik said firmly. "We'll catch him, and he'll pay for what he's done."

But Morgan wasn't so sure. She couldn't shake the feeling that the killer was always one step ahead of them, always taunting them with photos and clues just out of reach.

As the other officers arrived, Morgan stepped away from Owen's body. She knew what was coming next, the long process of documenting the scene and gathering evidence.

But for now, she just needed a moment to breathe.

***

Morgan sat in the passenger seat of Derik's car, alone, while she waited for him to finish up with the team. It was hard to stay resolute when they'd already lost so much, but she turned her focus to her phone as she tried to dig up more information on anything that could point them in the right direction.

Aaron Matthews was in custody, so there was no way he was the killer.

But they still had David Reed, the director Gloria had mentioned. She was exhausted, both physically and emotionally. The weight of Owen's death was crushing her, and the scars of her past failures were still too fresh.

But she couldn't give up

Looking up David Reed, she came across an article from a local film critic named Gerry Jensen. Jensen had written a scathing review of Reed's latest film, calling it a "violent and disturbing piece of garbage." The film was years old, but the review was written recently. Morgan clicked on the blog to see that Jensen had written many reviews about Reed's work, most of them critical, some of them with praise, particularly for his older stuff.

It seemed that Jensen had been both Reed's biggest fan, and biggest critic. A scan through his blog showed he was obsessed with surrealist films in general, clearly an expert on the topic. And his bio stated that he was located in town.

Morgan leaned back in the seat, her eyes fixed on the bright glow of her phone screen. She scrolled through Jensen's blog, reading his reviews of Reed's films with renewed interest. Jensen was clearly a film buff, but his reviews of Reed's work were different from the others. They were more passionate, almost personal. Morgan wondered if there was some kind of connection between Reed and Jensen.

Just then, Derik opened the driver's side door and slid into the seat next to her. "You alright?" he asked, concern etched onto his face.

Morgan nodded. "Yeah, I'm fine. Just... processing everything. Hey, check this out." She handed Derik the phone, and he frowned at the screen.

"David Reed again?"

"Not just him. Gerry Jensen, the film critic. This guy seems to be an expert on Reed's work, and strange films like this in general," Morgan said. "Maybe we can set up a meeting and have him examine the killer's films. He might be able to give us a clearer idea of who's making them."

Derik nodded thoughtfully. "It's a long shot, but it's worth a try, I guess. We're spinning our wheels in the mud here anyway."

Morgan smiled, feeling a glimmer of hope. "Exactly. And who knows, maybe he even knows something about Reed that could help us out."

Morgan leaned back in her seat, feeling the weight of this case heavy on her shoulders. The past twenty-four hours had been hell, and with the sun down, in truth, all she wanted was to rest and recharge.

But she couldn't do that.

Not yet.

There was too much work to be done, and with any luck, this film critic might point them in the right direction.

***

They arrived at Jensen's small apartment complex, and Morgan could tell just by looking at the shabby exterior that this was not a man who made a lot of money. She wondered what kind of person could be so passionate about strange and disturbing films, and how he would react to the idea of helping them with an active murder investigation.

Morgan had called Gerry on the way over, so he knew they were coming.

When they got upstairs, he answered the door quickly, his eyes darting between Morgan and Derik.

"Gerry Jensen?" Morgan asked, holding out her hand.

"That's me," he said, shaking her hand tightly.

"Thanks for agreeing to meet with us."

"Sure, I mean, it's not every day I get a call from the FBI," he said, chuckling softly to himself. "I'll help however I can. Please, come in. I've been waiting for someone to appreciate my knowledge of surrealism."

The apartment was small and cluttered, with stacks of DVDs and film posters covering almost every inch of the walls.

Morgan glanced around the room, noticing a few posters for Reed's films scattered around. "You seem to be quite the fan of David Reed's work," she said.

Jensen nodded eagerly. "Oh, yes. He's a genius, really. Some of his earlier films were absolutely mind-bending. But his more recent work before he dropped off the map has been... well, let's just say it's lost some of its magic."

Morgan couldn't help but wonder if there was more to Jensen's criticism than just artistic disagreement. "Do you know him personally?" she asked.

Jensen hesitated for a moment before nodding slowly. "Yes, we've met a few times. He's a very private person, though. Been years since I've seen him."

Morgan's curiosity piqued at the mention of Reed's reclusiveness. "Any idea why he dropped off the map?" she asked.

Jensen shrugged. "Not really. He was always a bit of a mystery. I heard rumors that he was working on something really big, something that was going to change the way people thought about film. But then he got fired from the film academy in town, and no one has heard from him or seen him since."

Morgan nodded, filing away the information for later. "Well, we were hoping you could help us with something. Gerry, I'm going to show you some footage," Morgan said, taking out her laptop and opening the file of the killer's latest film. "We're hoping you can help us identify the style or any themes that might point us towards the killer."

Morgan pressed play, and the film began. The same strange symbols and clips of animals hunting and insects feasting layered over images of the woman Owen had accidentally killed. Jensen watched the footage with interest, his eyes narrowing as he focused on the screen. After a few moments, he sat back in his chair.

"Well, that was certainly disturbing," Gerry said.

"But I must say, there's a clear influence of David Reed's earlier work here. Specifically, his film 'Aberration.' It's about a man who becomes obsessed with the idea that he's being watched, and the film is shot in a very surreal, almost dreamlike style. The use of animals and insects is a recurring motif throughout the film as well."

Morgan scribbled down the title of the film 'Aberration' in her notebook and looked back at Jensen. "That's helpful. Is there anything else you can tell us about this style of filmmaking?"

Jensen thought for a moment before nodding. "Well, it's clear that the creator is trying to make a statement with these films. I would guess that they're trying to express some kind of anger or frustration, perhaps with their own past or society in general. The use of violence and shock value is meant to provoke a response, to make people uncomfortable enough to pay attention. But beyond that, I couldn't say for certain. Surrealism is a complex and often deeply personal art form."

"Have you seen anything like this before? Any films or styles that this might resemble?"

Jensen thought for a moment, his eyes roaming around the room as if he were searching for an answer in the posters on the walls. "It's definitely surrealist. I can see some nods to Buñuel and Dali. But this feels more... primal, somehow. Less concerned with the abstract and more focused on the visceral. I've never seen anything quite like it, except in Reed's work."

"Do you think he could have made this?" Morgan asked, her heart in her throat.

Gerry sat on it, thinking. "Well, I do see a lot of potential influence," he said. "As for whether Reed himself made the film, I'm just not sure. Reed became more erratic near the end of his career and less consistent. It's possible. I will say, this does feel a bit too amateur for him."

Morgan nodded, feeling a sense of dread pool in the pit of her stomach. The idea that David Reed could be responsible for these grotesque and violent films was both terrifying and thrilling. It was a lead, at least, something that could potentially break the case wide open.

"Thank you, Gerry," Derik said, standing up from his seat. "This has been incredibly helpful."

Gerry smiled, looking pleased with himself. "Glad I could be of service."

As they were leaving, Morgan turned back to him. "One more thing. Do you have any idea where Reed might be? Any leads we could follow up on?"

Gerry hesitated for a moment before shaking his head. "I'm sorry, but I really don't. Reed was always very secretive, and he disappeared completely after he was fired from the academy. I wish I could be more help."

Morgan nodded, feeling a sense of disappointment. But she wasn't ready to give up yet. There had to be something else they could do.

Morgan thanked Gerry and left with Derik, her head swimming with possibilities. As they walked through the dark parking lot and back to the car, Morgan felt a chill run down her spine as she recalled the imagery on the film. It was all so deliberate. Could this whole thing be David Reed's return to the world of filmmaking? A disturbing art project?

Or was it someone just inspired by David's work?

Morgan couldn't be sure, but they needed to find Reed. They got back to Derik's car, and Morgan let out a sigh.

"Reed owns a lot of properties, but no one seems to know where he is," Morgan said. "But his daughter lives on the outskirts of town. If anyone knows where to find him, it's probably her. Maybe he's even living there."

"It's a good lead, Cross, but it's getting late." He sighed and rubbed his eyes. "I say we find a place to hunker in for the night and keep reviewing our files, then get some rest. The team could've found something new at the latest crime scene."

Morgan nodded in agreement, feeling the exhaustion hit her all at once. Her mind was still racing with the possibilities, but she knew Derik was right. They needed to rest and come back with a fresh perspective in the morning. Plus, she needed to feed her dog.

"Mind if we head to my place?" Morgan asked. "I've gotta feed Skunk and let him out."

"Sure thing, Cross," Derik said, starting the car and pulling out of the parking lot. "We'll pick up some food on the way."

Morgan smiled gratefully, feeling a sense of relief at the thought of being in her own space.

At the same time, her house was also the place where, last night, Darren La Roux had shown up, trying to kill her.

Morgan realized with dread that she'd never gotten rid of his gun.

CHAPTER FIFTEEN

Morgan eyed the garden next to her front door as she led Derik up the steps. Just last night, he'd come over and they'd talked about keeping things professional, but now everything felt different. The conversation with Gloria. Darren La Roux. Morgan's own secrets.

Somehow, everything had changed.

It was too risky right now to grab Darren's gun, which had been tossed into Morgan's garden. Not with Derik here. She hoped it would stay hidden until she had a moment to get it stashed somewhere. Until then, she unlocked her door and let Derik inside. Skunk barked happily and ran up to greet them at the door.

Morgan smiled at her furry friend and bent down to give him a pat. "Hey there, buddy. Did you miss me?"

Skunk wagged his tail and licked her hand. Morgan stood up and led Derik to the kitchen where she took out some bowls for the food they'd picked up. Neither of them had eaten, and Morgan knew Derik well enough to know he was always hungry.

"So, what's the plan for tomorrow?" Derik asked, leaning against the counter.

Morgan poured some kibble into Skunk's bowl and filled his water. "Well, first thing we'll do is head out to Reed's daughter's place and see if she knows anything. Then let's take it from there."

Without sustenance, she could barely think. She hoped their take-out would make her feel better.

Derik nodded, his eyes fixed on Morgan as she worked. "Yeah, that's a good idea. Maybe we can get some intel on Reed's whereabouts or what he's been up to. And in the meantime, we can keep digging into these films, see if we can find any connections."

Morgan grabbed a fork for each of them. She nodded in agreement.

Derik sighed and rubbed his temples. "It's all just so bizarre. There's so much to go through. I mean, I don't get why this guy is so obsessed with movies."

Morgan nodded, feeling the weight of the case on her shoulders. She passed Derik a hot bowl, and the two of them went into the living room to eat on the couch. Morgan's chest seized when she realized the coffee table was still out of place from her fight with Darren, but Derik didn't notice as she quietly fixed it.

The two sat down and began eating, and Morgan tried to shove the images of Darren in her house away.

"I was never really into movies," Derik went on. "I don't get the whole appeal. And the killer is so damn over the top with these films. I feel like he thinks he's making some kind of deep message, when really, it's just disturbing."

Morgan's mind wandered back to her life before she'd gone to prison. She had loved movies, once. Her dad used to bring her to them all the time. "My dad used to take me to theaters all the time," she said. "Including the drive-in from earlier."

"Ah." Derik nodded. "That was why you knew where it was."

"It was just a hunch," Morgan said, eating a tomato-covered noodle.

"But it was a good one," Derik said with a small smile. "You have a good mind for this stuff, Cross."

Morgan felt a warmth spread through her chest at his words, but also a twinge of guilt. She had been hiding so much from him. From everyone, really.

Thinking about the movies had her thinking about her dad, too. It still hurt that she'd been in prison when he passed away. She hadn't even been able to attend his funeral. Her dad had been the only one who had always been there for her, always visiting her in prison, always reminding her that she had someone on the outside waiting for her.

And yet he'd died before her sentence was even up.

"You okay?" Derik asked, and Morgan's eyes snapped to him.

"Yeah," she muttered, "just thinking about my dad."

"He was a good guy. I'm sorry you didn't get to say goodbye to him the proper way."

Morgan nodded, feeling a lump form in her throat. She took a swig of water to try and clear it. "Thanks, Derik. It still hurts, but I'm trying to keep going."

Derik reached over and put a hand on her knee. "We're here for you, Morgan. You don't have to do this alone."

Morgan felt a flutter in her stomach at his touch but tried to push it away. She needed to focus on the case. But it was hard to keep her mind on work when Derik was sitting so close to her, his warmth radiating off of him.

She finished her pasta and leaned back on the couch, looking at Derik. "Do you ever wonder what would've happened if you hadn't gone into the FBI?"

Derik chuckled. "Not really. I've always wanted to stop the bad guys, even when I was a kid. What about you?"

Morgan thought for a moment, then shook her head. "I never really had a plan. I just wanted to make the world a better place."

And what good had it done for her? Morgan had dedicated herself to the FBI, and yet someone had apparently betrayed her. She had confided in Derik about how she suspected someone in the FBI reported her the night that changed everything. The night a criminal had died, and Morgan had been blamed for their wrongful death.

Only Morgan hadn't killed anyone that night; it was her word against everyone else's.

"Maybe I'm not cut out for the FBI anymore anyway," Morgan said.

"What?" Derik scowled. "Morgan, you were made for this kind of work."

"Yeah, I know, but you don't know what it's like to feel like you can't trust your own shadow."

Derik's expression softened. "I may not know exactly what you're going through, but I can tell you this: you're not alone. You have me, and you have the team. We'll get to the bottom of this and clear your name."

Morgan let out a sigh. He didn't know how wrong he was. If Derik knew what had happened with Darren, how poorly she'd handled it, then she was sure he wouldn't have much faith left in her at all.

But right now, she couldn't bring herself to tell him. It was too risky. She had to keep her distance from him and protect him from her own mess. But for now, she would take comfort in his words. Derik's presence had always been one of the few things that could calm her down. She knew she could count on him to be there for her, even if she wasn't exactly sure how to be there for him in return.

Morgan leaned her head back against the couch and closed her eyes, feeling the weight of exhaustion and uncertainty settle in her bones. She tried to push away the thoughts of Darren, of her dad, of the case, but they all swirled around in her mind like a never-ending storm.

Derik finished his pasta and put his bowl down on the coffee table, then sat back on the couch beside her.

"Why don't you get some rest?" he suggested. "We have a big day tomorrow."

Morgan opened her eyes and looked at him. "I'm okay," she said, even though she knew she wasn't.

Derik shook his head. "No, you're not. You're exhausted. Go get some sleep, Morgan. I'll stay here and finish going through the files."

Morgan hesitated, then nodded. She did need to rest, but the awareness of Darren's gun in her garden was like a bomb. If Derik found it, she'd be screwed. Everything would fall apart.

She'd probably end up back in prison.

She had to move it.

"Sure," she said. "Let me just take Skunk out for a quick walk."

Skunk hopped up at the word, wagging his tail.

"You sure?" Derik asked. "I can take him. We get along well, don't we, boy?"

Skunk barked happily in return.

"No, really, it's okay," Morgan said. "I'll be right back. You stay here."

Morgan put Skunk's leash on and headed towards the door, hoping that she could move the gun without any trouble. She opened the door and stepped out into the cool night air, Skunk happily following her. Morgan made sure to keep an eye behind her, to make sure Derik wasn't watching through the windows, before leaning down into the garden and swiping up the gun. She quickly tucked it into her pants, hiding it underneath her clothes.

As she walked Skunk around the block, her mind raced with different scenarios. She thought about hiding the gun in a nearby dumpster, but that was too risky. What if someone found it and traced it back to her?

No, she needed a better plan.

She needed to get rid of the gun for good. She couldn't risk getting caught with it or anything leading back to her. As she walked, she spotted an abandoned lot on the corner of the street. The lot was overgrown with weeds and looked like it hadn't been touched in years.

Morgan thought about it for a moment before deciding it was the perfect spot. She could bury the gun deep in the ground, and no one would ever find it. She turned towards the lot, Skunk following her obediently.

Morgan reached the lot and quickly scanned the area. There was no one around, and the lot was deserted. She kneeled down and dug a small hole in the ground with her hands, making sure it was deep enough to hide the gun. She carefully wiped away her prints, then wrapped the gun in a plastic dog poop bag before burying it in the hole.

Satisfied with her work, Morgan covered the hole with dirt and stood up. She took a deep breath and wiped her hands on her pants, feeling relieved that the gun was no longer in her possession. If she needed to, she could easily make her way back here and dig it back up.

Until then, it was gone.

That was all that mattered.

Morgan made her way back to the house, feeling like a weight had been lifted off her shoulders. She opened the door and found Derik sitting on the couch, staring at the files in front of him.

He looked up as she entered. "Everything okay?"

Morgan nodded. "Yeah, everything's fine. Just needed some fresh air."

Derik stood up and stretched. "Alright, well, it's getting late. We should both get some rest."

Morgan agreed, feeling grateful for the escape from the anxiety that had been weighing on her. "You can crash on the couch if you want," Morgan said. "Then we can get right back to work in the morning."

Derik nodded before heading to the couch and getting comfortable. Morgan went to her bedroom, feeling relieved that the gun was no longer in her possession. She knew it wasn't a long-term solution, but it was the best she could do for now. She needed to focus on clearing her name and finding out who had betrayed her.

Morgan changed into her pajamas and crawled into bed, letting out a deep sigh. She closed her eyes, trying to clear her mind and fall asleep, but her thoughts kept swirling around in her head. She couldn't shake the feeling that she was being watched, that someone was always just around the corner, waiting to pounce on her.

She tossed and turned, unable to get comfortable, until finally, exhaustion took over and she fell into a deep sleep.

Morgan's dreams were filled with images of guns and betrayal.

Of people she thought she could trust turning on her.

CHAPTER SIXTEEN

Morning light seeped in through Morgan's curtains, pulling her from a dream. At the edge of her bed, Skunk whined, eager to be let out for a morning pee.

When the smell of coffee filled the air, memories of last night struck her.

Derik had stayed over on the couch.

Morgan sat up in bed, rubbing the sleep from her eyes. She knew they had a long day ahead of them, and she needed to get started. Morgan got out of bed, got dressed, and headed into the living room to find Derik already at work, pouring over files and sipping his coffee.

"Good morning," Morgan said as she walked over to him.

"Morning," Derik replied, not looking up from the papers in front of him. "I've been going over these files all morning. There's a lot of information to sift through."

Morgan sat down next to him, pouring herself a cup of coffee. "Have you found anything useful yet?"

Derik shook his head. "Not yet. I'm on board with you--we should go talk to Reed's daughter. But first, breakfast?"

Morgan forced a smile. She didn't have much of an appetite, her mind still focused on the gun buried in the lot. At the time, it had seemed like a good idea. But she needed to come up with a plan to get rid of it permanently. Someone could dig it up someday, and that could spell more trouble.

Once this case was over for good, then she would figure something out.

She sauntered toward the kitchen. "I don't have a whole lot of food, but what do you feel like? We should really get going."

Derik nodded in agreement. "Anything is fine, just something quick so we can get started on our day."

Morgan rummaged through her fridge, grabbing some eggs and bread. She quickly made them both some scrambled eggs and toast, placing the plates in front of them on the coffee table.

They ate in silence, Morgan lost in her thoughts and Derik focused on the files. She looked up at Derik, at the way the daylight filtered in through the window and brightened up his blue irises. Derik had always been good-looking, and her mind wandered back to what Gloria had said.

That he had been heartless.

Maybe he had been at one time, but perhaps the divorce from his ex-wife changed him. She had cheated on him, he'd said, and it had been traumatic. Something like that could change a man.

Morgan shook her head, trying to push those thoughts away. She needed to focus on the case, not her attraction to Derik. They finished breakfast and got ready to head out.

Derik drove as they navigated through the city under the morning light, toward the mansion on the outskirts of town where David Reed's daughter allegedly lived. The sun rising in the sky cast a brilliant gold and orange hue over the cityscape, a contrast to yesterday's overcast sky. Today would be sunny, as it turned out.

Morgan could only hope it was a sign that things were about to look up.

They couldn't afford to find any more victims.

If David Reed was the killer, then Morgan hoped they could track him down and bring him to justice soon.

As they pulled into the driveway of the mansion, Morgan couldn't help but feel a sense of unease. The mansion was grand, with a long driveway and perfectly manicured lawn, but it gave off an eerie vibe. The windows were dark and foreboding, with no signs of life inside.

Derik parked the car, and they both got out, making their way towards the front door. Morgan could feel her heart pounding in her chest as they waited for a response. After a few moments, they heard footsteps approaching, and the door opened to reveal a young woman in her early twenties.

"Hi, can I help you?" The woman's voice was timid, and she looked like she was about to bolt.

Morgan stepped forward, flashing her badge. "We're with the FBI. Are you Ellie Reed?"

The woman's eyes widened, but she nodded. "Yes, that's me. What's this about?"

"We wanted to talk to you about your father, David," Morgan said.

Ellie's eyes widened, and she stepped aside, allowing them to enter. The mansion was just as grand on the inside, with high ceilings and ornate decorations. But there was something off about the place. It was too quiet, too still. Morgan noticed a variety of surrealist art adorning the walls of the house, ranging from abstract paintings to sculptures and installations. Along with these, she observed glossy posters of David's movies plastered across the walls. She could feel a strange energy emanating from the artwork, as if it was a window into a different world.

Morgan and Derik followed Ellie into a sitting room, where she gestured for them to take a seat on a plush couch. She remained standing, clearly nervous.

"What's this about?" she asked, wringing her hands. "Have you... have you seen my father?"

"No, we haven't," Morgan said, shifting her weight on the couch. "We were hoping you could help shed some light on where we might be able to find him."

"Oh, no," Ellie said, bowing her head with sadness. "I haven't seen my father in years. He... disappeared."

"Disappeared?" Morgan lifted a brow. "Did you report him missing?" There was nothing of that in David's file.

"No, because he's still out there." Ellie went over to the bookshelf and pulled out a box. Nervously, she placed it on the coffee table and opened it.

Inside were several letters.

Ellie plucked one out and handed it to Morgan. "This is the most recent one. He sends them monthly, to let me know he is still around, but I never know where they're from."

Morgan took the letter, scanning it quickly. It was written in a shaky hand, revealing little information beyond the fact that David was still alive and on the run. "What do you think he's running from?" she asked, handing the letter back to Ellie.

"I don't know," Ellie said, shaking her head. "He was always a private person, but he never hurt anyone. He loved me and my mother, but he was always distant, like he was carrying a burden. He put his heart and soul into his art. I know it's... very strange to most people, but he has quite the following, as I'm sure you know."

"Do you think he's still making movies, wherever he is?" Morgan asked.

"I'm sure he is," Ellie said. "This is his handwriting, so I know it's him."

Morgan nodded. All this did was prove David was most likely alive. It didn't prove that he wasn't nearby, killing people and making his twisted films.

"My father was kind," Ellie said, her eyes glazing over. "He is kind. Wherever he is..."

"But he walked out on you," Derik said. "Doesn't that make you angry?"

"Sometimes," Ellie said. "But he was always very strange. I know losing his job at the academy was a big deal for him. He loved it there. He loved teaching, but the school deemed his work too obscure, and so he faded from memory. I think he mostly made himself fade away."

Morgan observed Ellie's expression, noticing the sadness in her eyes. She could see that Ellie was still holding onto hope, despite her father's disappearance.

"Ellie, we need you to think carefully," Morgan said. "Has your father ever exhibited any violent behavior? Has he ever made any threatening statements or gestures towards anyone?"

Ellie shook her head. "No, never. He was always just...different. He had his own way of doing things, but he was never harmful."

Morgan exhaled softly. If Ellie was telling the truth, then David Reed may not be the killer they were chasing. But she couldn't shake the feeling that there was more to this story than what Ellie was telling them.

She decided that their best bet was to just show Ellie the film and see what she thought. Gerry, the film critic, had thought it was possible this could be David's work, but at the same time, he mentioned it was a bit too amateur as well. Maybe David's own daughter would know his signature style better than anyone.

"Ellie, we need to show you something," Morgan said, taking out her laptop from her bag. "It might be difficult to watch, but it's important."

Ellie looked at the laptop apprehensively but nodded her agreement. Morgan opened her laptop and pulled up the video. Derik and Ellie crowded around the screen as the film started.

Morgan watched Ellie's face as the film played. Her expression was hard to read, but there was a hint of recognition there. Finally, the film ended, and Ellie turned to face them.

"That was... odd," she said. "It seems inspired by my father's work."

"We thought so too," Morgan said, feeling validated. "But do you think your father made it?"

Ellie's brows pinched. "Well, no, I wouldn't say this is his work at all."

Morgan's heart sank. If this wasn't David's work, then who was behind it all? Was there another twisted mind out there, making these horrifying films and killing innocent people?

Ellie must have noticed Morgan's disappointment because she quickly added, "But it does have some elements that resemble his work. The use of color and the surrealism, that's definitely something my father would do. But the execution is completely wrong."

Morgan felt a pang of disappointment. So much for that lead. "Why do you say that?" she asked, hoping to get some more information.

"It's too...crass," Ellie said, searching for the right words. "My father's work was always avant-garde, but it had a certain elegance to it. This is just...gross. It's like it's trying too hard to shock you without any real substance. And the violence- my father was never interested in depicting violence in that way. It's almost...amateurish, if I'm being honest."

Morgan nodded, scribbling down notes. "I see."

"But..."

Morgan's eyes flitted to Ellie's. She bit her lip as she said, "It does somewhat remind me of one of my father's students."

"His student?" Morgan asked, trading a concerned look with Derik.

She prayed this wasn't another dead-end.

"Yes," Ellie replied, nodding her head. "My father had a student named Adam. He was always a bit strange, even by my father's standards. He would often come to our house to discuss art and filmmaking with my father, but he always gave off an eerie vibe. My father was his mentor for a while, but they had a falling out. I don't know the details, and my father never spoke of him again, but that didn't stop Adam from contacting him. Honestly, he seemed a bit obsessed. It concerned me."

Morgan's heart quickened at the mention of Adam. Could he be the one behind all of this carnage?

"Do you know where we could find this Adam?" Morgan asked, trying to keep her tone even.

"I'm not sure," Ellie said. "His name was Adam McCormack, though, and he lived across town. He used to drive all the way across the city just to pester my father."

"And this falling out was before he got fired from the school," Derik clarified.

"That's right," Ellie said.

"Do you have any idea what caused the falling out between them?" Morgan asked, trying to gather as much information as possible about Adam.

"No, I don't," Ellie said, shaking her head. "My father never told me. But I do remember him being upset for several days after they had a disagreement."

Morgan nodded, jotting down notes about Adam McCormack. If what Ellie was saying was true, then they could be dealing with an obsessed fan of David Reed's work, hence the similarities.

It would all make sense.

But they needed to find this Adam before they could draw any conclusions and see if he fit the profile of the killer.

***

According to the database, Adam McCormack never moved from his place across the city, but it was a long drive.

Morgan could tell Derik was less than eager to make it as they dealt with the morning traffic. She sat in the passenger seat holding a fresh cup of coffee, as they'd just stopped to grab a cup to keep them going through the morning. This Adam McCormack lead could be huge, but there were no guarantees. Morgan had been doing this for long enough to know that.

According to his file, which Morgan read as Derik drove, Adam McCormack grew up underprivileged, but had earned a scholarship to the film academy.

His life before that had been a series of rather unfortunate events, though.

For one, Adam's parents had been shot and killed during a break-in at their mobile home. Morgan realized it was the same mobile home Adam now lived in.

He'd never moved away.

That was more than enough to traumatize someone, to turn them to violence.

"McCormack had a rough life," Morgan commented, and Derik glanced at her as he drove.

"Oh yeah? What happened?"

"His parents were shot and killed right before his eyes during a break-in."

Derik let out a low whistle. "That's a tough break."

"That it is," Morgan agreed. "I can't help but wonder if that's what pushed him over the edge. Losing his parents like that, and then having a falling out with his mentor. It's sad, really. But I can't help but wonder if he's taken his trauma and turned it into something...darker."

As they drove on, Morgan suddenly saw the brake lights ahead of them. Derik hit the brakes hard, and Morgan's coffee spilled all over her blouse.

"Dammit!" she cursed, pulling the fabric away from her chest so it wouldn't burn. But the hot liquid still seeped onto her skin, immediately burning.

"Damn, sorry, Cross," Derik said. "They got me out of nowhere."

Morgan gritted her teeth, feeling the heat of the coffee seeping through her clothes. She hadn't packed a change of clothes, and she could already tell this was going to be a long day. She didn't want to go through her day with coffee all over her blouse; that sounded like a good way to not be taken seriously by suspects and colleagues.

"We should probably stop by my house so I can change," Morgan said, trying not to sound as exasperated as she felt. "It's only a few blocks away from here."

Derik glanced in the rear-view mirror before slowly making his way over to the right lane and nodding. "Yeah, you're right, that's probably best."

"And you can walk my dog to make it up to me," Morgan muttered, annoyed. All she wanted was to get to Adam's house, but they were at yet another impasse.

But it was fine, she reminded herself.

They knew who Adam was now.

And they would get to him soon enough.

CHAPTER SEVENTEEN

He watched the other man from afar.

It was a quiet neighborhood, nice and suburban, and the man looked so domestic as he walked the Pitbull down the street.

A good Samaritan, on the surface.

But he knew the truth.

The man was no hero. Not the way he presented himself.

From his position up the street, he pulled out his camera and zoomed in, taking a video of the man and the dog, plus a few snapshots.

He knew he was taking a risk, but it was a risk he was willing to take. He had been following the man for some time, watching him, learning his patterns. Just as he'd done with the others.

He had become quite good at this game, his obsession with the truth fueling him. He had always been this way, even as a child, questioning everything and never taking things at face value. But as he got older, that questioning turned into something darker, a need to uncover the ugliness that most people tried to hide.

As he watched the man with the Pitbull, he knew that there was something about him that didn't quite add up. The man seemed too perfect, too put-together. And with each passing day, the man's façade was starting to crack. The man was hiding something from the world.

But he knew what it was.

He tucked the camera away and followed the man and his Pitbull, staying hidden in the shadows all the while. He knew that the truth about this man needed to come to light, and he was the one who was going to make it happen.

To make him pay.

To watch him in his final moments, reliving the horrors of all he'd done, all those he'd hurt.

He'd deserve it.

They all did.

That was why they got the honor of being the sole viewers of his precious films. And this man?

He had no idea the art he was going to witness soon.

As he followed the man, he couldn't help but feel a sense of excitement building within him. He knew he was getting closer and closer to the moment of truth. The moment when he would finally be able to reveal the man's true nature to the world.

The man continued to walk down the street, seemingly unaware of the danger that was lurking in the shadows.

But that was fine. He was safe, for now.

He wasn't out on a hunt yet. Right now, he was only gathering intel. Evidence. Proof.

He continued to follow the man and his dog, taking mental notes of everything he could see. The way the man walked, the way he held the leash, the way he spoke to the dog. He was observing every detail, every nuance, looking for any sign of weakness that he could exploit.

It wasn't long before the man stopped in front of a house, disappearing inside.

A house that wasn't his.

He waited, watching the house intently as his plan brewed in his mind.

Yes, it was all coming together.

His greatest film yet.

In fact, he couldn't help but feel like, maybe, showing only one person would be a waste.

For the first time ever, he wondered to himself; what would it be like to sell out a whole theater?

CHAPTER EIGHTEEN

Morgan slammed her fist against Adam McCormack's door, grateful to finally be there after their short intermission. She was in a clean blouse, and Skunk had been walked by Derik, who now stood by her side, his anxiety just as palpable as hers.

Except Adam never answered.

The house was more like a mobile home on the outskirts of town, truly in the middle of nowhere. It was a rough neighborhood. The mobile home had faded and chipped walls, peeling paint, and a broken window that had been hastily boarded up. The roof was missing shingles in some places, and the yard was overgrown with weeds. There were numerous graffiti markings on the sides of the house, and the surrounding area was filled with garbage and debris. The air was thick with an oppressive atmosphere, as though no one dared to step out at night.

There was also no car here.

"I guess he's out," Derik said.

On the drive over, Morgan had learned more about Adam McCormack. For one, he had dropped out of school, presumably after his falling out with David Reed. Secondly, he didn't have a job and was collecting welfare, which meant he didn't have many places to go.

"We could wait for him to come back," Morgan said. "The guy is unemployed, so he should be returning soon."

"I don't know, Cross. I wanna talk to the guy too, but can we really waste our day staking out his house? Let's get an officer to do it and go see if the team has uncovered anything else from Owen's crime scene."

Morgan sighed, glancing at the house. She peered through the windows and saw no sign of life. As much as she hated to admit it, Derik was right. They could easily have an officer watching the place in case Adam came back.

"Fine," she said, reluctantly. "Let's head back to the station. But I want to make sure we have someone keeping an eye on this place."

Derik nodded in agreement, and they headed back to their car, the feeling of disappointment heavy on their shoulders.

As they drove back to the station, Morgan couldn't help but feel frustrated. They were so close, yet so far. They had a name, a suspect, but they still didn't have any solid evidence to tie him to the murders. It was like chasing after a ghost.

She shook her head, trying to clear her thoughts. They couldn't give up now. They had come too far to let it all slip away.

When they arrived back at HQ, there was a flustered-looking man pacing around out front. Derik parked the car, and they got out. Morgan thought nothing of the man, although he clearly didn't work here or with the FBI.

But as they approached, the man's eyes flicked up to meet Morgan's, and she felt a chill run down her spine. There was something off about him, something that made her uneasy.

"Can I help you?" she asked, her voice authoritative. Derik was right behind her.

The man looked at her, his eyes glinting with a strange intensity. "Are you the ones in charge of the case with the films? Cross and Greene?"

"What?" Morgan scowled. The case hadn't been released to the news. "How the hell do you know about that?"

The man's face reddened. "I'm Bella Hunt's father."

Morgan's stomach dropped, and she shared a concerned look with Derik. Bella Hunt. That was the girl Owen Fernandez had accidentally killed.

"I heard he's dead," Mr. Hunt said. "Fernandez. The bastard who killed my little girl."

"How did you get details on this?" Derik asked, crossing his arms.

"Let's just say his wife felt guilty and like she owed me a damn favor for what her husband did to my little girl," said Mr. Hunt.

Morgan didn't have time for this. She felt for Mr. Hunt's loss, but she didn't know what he wanted. "I'm sorry, Mr. Hunt, but we need to keep working."

They attempted to move past him, but Mr. Hunt blocked their path.

Morgan squared her shoulders, meeting the man's enraged eyes.

"I want to see the tape," he said. "There was a tape with my Bella on it, and I want to see it."

"That's confidential evidence," Morgan said, trying to brush past him again.

Mr. Hunt blocked her once more.

The hostility rose in the air like a flame.

Morgan could feel her adrenaline kick in, her instincts telling her to be ready for anything. She could see Derik tensing up beside her, ready to intervene if necessary.

"Mr. Hunt, I understand your frustration," Morgan began, in a calm yet firm tone. "But we can't just let anyone view the evidence in an ongoing investigation."

"I don't give a damn about your investigation!" Mr. Hunt shouted. "All I care about is seeing the tape of my daughter. I deserve to know what happened to the bastard who killed my daughter!"

Morgan felt her patience beginning to wear thin. She understood that Mr. Hunt was grieving, but they couldn't just show him evidence like that. It was against protocol.

"I'm sorry, Mr. Hunt, but we can't just show you evidence like that," Morgan said firmly. "It's against protocol."

"I don't care about your damn protocol," Mr. Hunt spat, his eyes blazing with anger. "My daughter was on that tape, and I have a right to see it. You owe me that much."

Morgan could feel the tension in the air as the situation escalated. She knew they needed to diffuse the situation before it got out of hand.

"Look, Mr. Hunt, I understand that you're upset," Morgan said softly. "But showing you the tape isn't going to bring your daughter back. We're doing everything we can to bring justice to the victims, including your daughter. I'm sorry, but we can't just-"

But before Morgan could finish, Mr. Hunt lunged at her with surprising speed, his hands reaching for her throat.

Morgan reacted quickly, sidestepping his attack, and grabbing onto his arm. She twisted it behind his back and pushed him against the wall of the building.

"Get off me, you bitch!" Mr. Hunt screamed, struggling to break free.

Derik rushed forward to help cuff the man while Morgan held him in place.

"What the hell is your problem, pal?" Morgan demanded. "Attacking a federal agent on government property? Are you asking to go to jail?"

Mr. Hunt continued to thrash and curse, but Derik managed to get handcuffs on him. Morgan stepped back, straightening her jacket, and trying to shake off the adrenaline that was still pulsing through her veins. Mr. Hunt was like a caged animal, frothing at the mouth.

"Whatever this is really about," Morgan said, "I hope it was worth it."

Mr. Hunt spat at her feet, and Morgan shoved him in the direction of the building.

***

It turned out that Francis Hunt, Bella's father, had a long history of criminal behavior.

Violence, mostly, but that didn't surprise Morgan. She read everything she could about him as he waited in the interrogation room, and even though Morgan could see he had a long list of assaults, she didn't understand why he'd snapped at her like that.

It was all so risky.

Morgan stood outside of the interrogation room with Derik. Before they went in, she said, "You don't think he was involved in Owen's murder, do you?"

Derik's jaw tightened. "I don't know. He clearly had the motive to want Owen dead, and he's clearly going through a mental break."

It was true; no one had more motive to kill Owen than Mr. Hunt, but his motives wouldn't explain the other victims.

"What about the others?" Morgan asked. "It doesn't add up. And why would he just give himself to us like this?"

"Maybe he wanted to get caught," Derik said. "Maybe Owen was his final kill, and now he's realized he has nothing left to do."

Morgan nodded, thinking it over. "True. If he had a mental break, he could have started killing other people as a means of vengeance, then finished off with the one he really wanted to kill."

Derik nodded, agreement written on his face. "We won't know for sure until we get more evidence. But for now, we need to focus on getting a confession out of him."

Morgan took a deep breath, steeling herself for what would come next. Interrogating a suspect was never easy, but it was even more complicated when they were emotionally volatile.

They entered the room, and Mr. Hunt glared at them from across the table. His hands were cuffed to the metal chair, and he looked like a wild animal in a cage.

105

Morgan took a deep breath, trying to remain calm.

"Mr. Hunt," she said, her voice stern. "You just assaulted a federal agent. Do you understand the severity of your actions?"

"I just want to see the tape," Mr. Hunt said, his voice shaking.

"Why?" Derik asked. "Why was it so important for you to come here and ask to see the tape?"

Mr. Hunt's eyes flickered with a sudden fear, and he looked away from Derik's gaze. Morgan noticed the shift in his demeanor, and her intuition kicked in. She leaned forward, putting on her empathetic face.

"Mr. Hunt, we know you're going through a difficult time, and we want to help you," Morgan said. "But in order for us to do that, we need to understand why you're so desperate to see that tape."

Mr. Hunt hesitated, his eyes darting around the room. Finally, he spoke in a low voice.

"I...I didn't want to believe it," he said. "But when I saw the news reports about Owen Fernandez's death, I had a sick feeling in my gut. Then his wife told me about you FBI agents and something about a film with my daughter's face on it, and I had to know the truth. If someone killed him, was it really because of what he did to Bella?"

Morgan leaned back in her chair, considering Mr. Hunt's words. The man's desperation was palpable, and it reminded her of the countless other families she had seen in the same position. Grief could drive people to do crazy things.

But something in Mr. Hunt's story wasn't adding up. If he was truly innocent, why had he attacked her when she denied him access to the evidence?

"Why would you attack me, Mr. Hunt?" Morgan asked, her tone even.

Mr. Hunt looked up at her, his eyes darkening. "I was angry, Agent. I lost my daughter, and then you tell me I can't even see the evidence that could help me understand what happened to her killer? My emotions got the best of me. I'm sorry."

Morgan raised an eyebrow, not entirely convinced. But she knew there was only one way to get to the truth.

"Mr. Hunt, we need to know if you had anything to do with Owen Fernandez's murder," Morgan said, her voice firm. "You had motive, and your violent history makes you a prime suspect."

Mr. Hunt's eyes widened, and for a moment, Morgan thought she saw a flash of guilt in them. But then he shook his head vehemently.

"I didn't kill anyone!" he shouted. "Believe me, I wish I had. But I didn't. He deserved to pay for what he did to Bella. I need to know if it was really about her. If it was, then maybe I could sleep at night."

Morgan could see the pain etched on Mr. Hunt's face, and for a moment, she felt a pang of sympathy. Losing a child was one of the worst things a human being could go through.

"Mr. Hunt," she said, her voice softening. "I understand that you're hurting, but we need to determine the truth about what happened to Owen Fernandez. You've been through a lot, and we're here to help you. But you need to help us too. Did you have anything to do with his murder?"

Mr. Hunt shook his head again. "No. I didn't. I swear."

Morgan opened her mouth to speak again when the door opened, and none other than AD Mueller poked his head in, his expression dark and angry.

Morgan's stomach bottomed out.

Derik shot her a frown, but Morgan was clueless. She had no idea why AD Mueller was interrupting their interrogation, but she had a feeling it had something to do with her.

Her blood froze over.

What if...

What if it was about Darren?

"Cross," Mueller said, "I need to talk to you in my office. Alone."

CHAPTER NINETEEN

Morgan's heart raced as she followed AD Mueller into his office. Her mind raced with possibilities of what he could want to talk to her about. It had to be serious to interrupt their interrogation with Mr. Hunt.

Once they were inside, Mueller shut the door and turned to her, his eyes hard.

"Cross," he said, his voice low and dangerous. Morgan's chest filled with nerves. She tried to stay strong, but she couldn't shake the feeling that everything was about to topple over on her head.

She couldn't go back to prison.

Never again.

But then Mueller said, "You remember Clancy Smith."

For a moment, Morgan let out a breath of relief.

It wasn't about Darren.

But then more dread filled her to the brim because Clancy Smith-- this was bad too.

Mueller had already known that Morgan had been caught meeting with him. Someone had taken photos of her. All Mueller knew was that Clancy was a drug addict, not the real reason why Morgan was meeting with him, which was actually because of Samson. The Seven Signs Killer had given Clancy's name to Morgan, and Clancy had told her information about the alleged agent who may have betrayed her the night that she was accused of murder. The night that led to her arrest, and her spending ten years--wrongfully--behind bars.

"What about him?" Morgan asked.

"He croaked, Cross," Mueller said. "He was arrested for some drug charges, and he gave you up to get a lighter sentence. I know why you were meeting with him."

Morgan gritted her teeth. "And why was that?"

"Because you can't let go of the past," Mueller said. "Because you're trying to work with lowlife criminals to try and get information about your arrest, but you know what, Cross? What happened to you, happened, and you can't get those ten years back."

Morgan's jaw tightened more. Mueller had some damn nerve.

"But you're back with the FBI," Mueller said, "and we have a reputation to uphold. You can't just be meeting with petty criminals in the night like this. And to lie to me about it--it's too much, Cross."

Morgan took a deep breath, trying to keep her emotions in check. She knew Mueller was right - she couldn't let her past consume her. But at the same time, she couldn't just let go of what had happened to her. Not when there was still a chance to clear her name.

"I understand, sir," Morgan said, her voice calm. "I had my reasons for meeting with Clancy, but I should have been upfront with you about it. It won't happen again."

Mueller studied her for a moment, his expression unreadable. Then: "You're right, it won't. You're suspended until further notice, Cross. Give me your gun and badge."

Morgan's heart sank as she reached for her gun and badge and handed them over to Mueller. She had worked so hard to regain her position in the FBI, and now it was all slipping away.

"I understand," she said again, her voice barely above a whisper.

Mueller nodded curtly. "You can go now, Cross."

Morgan turned to leave, her mind numb.

It was all so cold.

Mueller was cutting her just like that, a suspension so soon after she'd been hired back.

It wasn't right.

And yet Morgan didn't have it in her to react.

She didn't have it in her to fight.

Because the truth was, she didn't trust the FBI anymore. She didn't know who was on her side or who was working behind her back. For all she knew, Mueller had betrayed her too.

As she walked out of Mueller's office, Morgan's mind was racing with thoughts of everything that had brought her to this moment. The years she spent in prison, the betrayal of her colleagues, and now this. It was all too much to handle.

She walked out of the office, her mind numb, and headed toward her own office like a zombie so she could collect her things.

As she gathered her belongings, she couldn't help but feel like all hope was lost. She had no job, no evidence to clear her name, and a growing distrust for the FBI. But then a small voice in her head reminded her that she still had one thing - her determination. She wouldn't let anyone or anything stand in the way of her quest for the truth.

With renewed resolve, Morgan made a decision. She couldn't rely on anyone else to help her, so she would have to do it all on her own. She would gather evidence, talk to witnesses, and follow every lead until she finally found out what really happened on the night of her arrest. To hell with the FBI.

If Mueller wanted to suspend her, then fine.

All that meant was that she had no obligation to play by his rules anymore.

Just then, a knock at the door. Derik rushed in, his face urgent.

"Oh, thank God you're still here," he said.

Morgan barely looked at him. "Why aren't you with Hunt?"

"I confirmed his alibi," Derik said, "it's not him. Mueller said you're suspended? What the hell is going on?"

"Yeah, for the Clancy thing," Morgan said shortly. "Forget it, Derik. It's over."

"Like hell it is."

Derik's voice was fierce. "I'm not going to let you give up, Morgan. I know you might not trust the FBI, but you can trust me. Let me help you."

Morgan looked at him, studying his face. She knew Derik was sincere and always had her back, but she couldn't take the risk of dragging him down with her.

"I appreciate it, Derik," she said finally, "but this is something I have to do on my own."

"Don't be ridiculous," Derik said, his voice firm. "You shouldn't have to face this alone."

"I'm not alone," Morgan said, a small smile tugging at the corners of her lips. "I have Skunk waiting for me at home. He's a good dog."

"Come on, be serious."

Morgan sighed, stuffing her last item into her bag. She met Derik's concerned blue gaze. She didn't get why he even bothered to care about having her around.

"It's not my call," Morgan said. "If Mueller wants me gone, then I'm gone. To hell with the FBI."

"But what about the case?"

Morgan paused. Maybe she was just as done with the FBI as they were with her, but Derik was right--one thing she wasn't done with was this case.

They'd worked too hard, gotten too close. Adam McCormack was still out there, waiting to be found and questioned.

Mueller couldn't just cut Morgan out mid-case. It wasn't right.

And yet he'd done it.

"It doesn't matter," Morgan said. "Mueller made his call, and I'm not gonna fight him on it. He wants me out, Derik."

"But I don't." Derik stepped closer to her, and Morgan's heart pounded. "Don't leave me hanging. You and I both know you're the only one who can finish this case with me."

Morgan could hardly believe what she was hearing. Derik had always been more by the books than she had. "What, you want me to work with you behind Mueller's back?"

"If you don't do anything reckless or stupid, then yeah," Derik said. "I need your brain on this, Cross."

Morgan hesitated, her mind racing. She knew it was a bad idea to go behind the FBI's back, but she also knew that Derik was right. They had worked too hard on this case to just let it go. And deep down, she wanted nothing more than to clear her name and bring the killer down.

At the same time, if Morgan couldn't be reckless and stupid, then maybe she was no use to Derik anyway. He wanted her to work off the books, while also following his rules. Not Mueller's, but Derik's.

Morgan had to admit, she wanted to keep working on this case, but she wanted to do it her own way. She didn't need Derik getting caught in the crossfire; she already felt enough guilt when it came to him. For her own lashing out. And for having feelings for him when he probably could never return them.

"I'm sorry, Derik," Morgan said, "but I'm out. You can work this on your own. I believe in you."

Of course, she had no intention of backing off, but she needed Derik to believe she was leaving it alone. At least for now.

Once she found information her own way, she'd call him.

"Cross, c'mon," Derik said, his voice hurt.

But Morgan didn't look back as she left the office. She had a plan, and it didn't involve Derik or the FBI.

She was going to find the evidence she needed, and no one was going to stand in her way.

CHAPTER TWENTY

Derik couldn't believe this was happening.

As he sat in his office at HQ, he could feel the absence of Morgan all around him. It had felt like they were finally getting somewhere and then, out of nowhere, she was gone.

He'd been working all day, and now it was well into the night. The good news: there hadn't been another murder. The bad: he was nowhere near closer to finding the killer.

To make matters worse, Adam McCormack, the only lead he and Morgan had before she'd been suspended, was still missing. No one had seen him.

So, Derik sat alone in his office, drinking tea to keep himself awake, buried in case files, trying to draw some sort of connection between the victims that might lead to who the killer could be. But he felt like he was spinning his wheels in the mud. And without Morgan to help him work through these theories, he was even more distracted and lost.

He couldn't help but feel like he had failed her. Failed to convince her to stay and fight.

Or maybe he should have stood up to AD Mueller more. Told him to see the humanity in what Morgan did.

Anyone would want to understand why they'd lost ten years of their life.

But Derik couldn't control Morgan; he could only control how he handled this without her. Morgan had been sure that Adam McCormack was a solid lead. The least Derik could do was look into him, to try and find some clue to truly link him to the case.

Online, Adam had no social media presence at all, at least not listed publicly. He wondered if he had an anonymous account. Someone as theatrical as the killer, who loved attention and filmmaking, was unlikely to not seek attention online, in Derik's mind. But how could he prove it?

He supposed he could get tech to check Adam's IP address. Maybe someone far more tech-savvy could dig something up.

Maybe it was a reach, but he had to try something.

So, with a sigh, Derik packed up his things and headed to the tech lab. It was an unorthodox approach, sure, but if anyone could find something in Adam's online footprint, it was the geniuses at the tech lab. After all, they were paid to be detectives with their computers.

In the tech lab, Derik found himself surrounded by dozens of computer screens, but most of the personnel had gone home by now.

He approached one of the remaining techs, a young guy named Ethan, and explained his situation, asking if they could help him locate any possible anonymous accounts belonging to Adam McCormack. Ethan nodded and got to work.

Derik watched as Ethan's fingers flew over the keyboard, pulling up information from various databases and search engines.

"Got it," Ethan said, turning to Derik with a grin. "Someone at this IP addresses has an anonymous account under the handle @filmfreak_89. Been active for over a year now."

Derik couldn't believe it. They had a lead, finally.

"Can you pull up the account?" Derik asked. "Does it have any videos? We're looking for someone with knack for strange, surreal films."

Ethan nodded and began to type furiously. The screen in front of him flickered to life, showing a page with a black background and white text. The handle @filmfreak_89 was emblazoned at the top, and underneath it was a long list of videos with titles like "The Puppet Master," "The Dreamer," and "The Dark One." Derik's heart sank as he realized that he had over a year's worth of content to comb through. But if it meant finding a clue to help catch the killer, it was worth it.

"Can you sort these by date?" Derik asked, gesturing at the list of videos.

Ethan nodded and clicked a few buttons. The list rearranged itself, with the newest videos appearing at the top.

Ethan clicked play, and familiar imagery filled the screen.

Animals hunting.

Insects feasting.

And a symbol...

That symbol.

Derik's stomach fell to the floor as the realization hit him over the back of the head.

This film was just like the killer's.

***

Derik's car was a black silhouette under the night sky in the parking lot. The clouds were rolling in, obscuring the moon, and painting the sky in layers of darkness. The wind picked up, sending a chill through the air that made Derik shiver as he ran towards his car.

He pressed his phone to his ear and called Morgan, but the phone rang and rang, and she didn't pick up.

"Damn it, Cross, where are you?" he asked.

He reached his car and dug into his pocket for his keys, but he didn't immediately feel them.

He searched his pockets again, patting down the inside of each one and checking his bag, but still found nothing. Derik cursed under his breath as he realized what had happened. He had left his keys at the tech lab; he must have dropped them during all the excitement.

Frustration coursed through him, and Derik turned back to the building. What was wrong with him? Was he really this lost without Morgan on the case? He'd been a fine FBI agent for ten years without her, but something about this case felt so off without her, like it was her case, and he was just tagging along, but now he had to take charge.

As he walked back toward the building, he caught a gleam of something on the concrete.

His keys.

They were right there.

Feeling foolish, Derik knelt down and grabbed them, then flicked the fob to unlock his car. He was being an idiot.

But he couldn't help it. The stress of the investigation and Morgan's suspension was getting to him. His mind was racing with possibilities, but he could feel himself getting closer to the killer.

He got into his car and took a breath, trying to calm his mind, comforted by the silence he was now trapped within. Sighing, he glanced at his reflection in the rear-view mirror.

And that was when he saw it.

A person, sitting in the backseat of his car, their face shielded by a black hood.

Derik's blood ran cold.

Before he could react, a bag was pulled over his head, and Derik's world fell into darkness.

CHAPTER TWENTY ONE

Morgan crept into the film academy, checking over her shoulder to see if she'd been followed.

She hadn't.

A long, empty hall stretched behind her, so she focused forward, her sights set on one destination: the school's records.

More specifically, Adam McCormack's records.

As planned, Morgan had no intention of letting this case go. Derik would never condone her breaking into a school like this, but she hadn't technically broken in; she'd had Gloria let her in under the guise of work, then said she was leaving, when really, she was making her way to the opposite wing of the school.

Morgan's heart was pounding with anticipation as she made her way down the deserted hallway. She had to find something, anything, that could link Adam to the murders. If she could just find a clue, maybe she could convince Derik--and the FBI--that Adam was, without a doubt, the killer. It was a lot to bet on, but Morgan was sure she could find evidence.

As she rounded a corner, a door caught her eye.

Finally, she reached the records room, and she pushed open the door, stepping into a small, cramped space filled with filing cabinets. She quickly made her way to the section marked M, then dug through until she found "McCormack, Adam," and began rifling through the files.

Most of them were simple school records. Adam had been a good student, apparently, and he was in every one of David Reed's classes. A folder marked "Film Club" had a sticky note on it that read "Adam McCormack" in bold letters.

Morgan's heart raced as she opened the folder and began to read.

Inside were handwritten notes detailing Adam's involvement in the film club, including a list of all the club members and their roles. Morgan scanned the list, searching for any familiar names or connections to the case. Nothing yet.

She kept looking, realizing that a physical file was unlikely to contain the evidence she needed. She wanted to know about the videos Adam had made for class.

She read one teacher's report, from after David Reed was fired. A new teacher. It read:

"Mr. McCormack utilizes violent imagery and symbolism in his work, which some students find repugnant and reminiscent of Professor Reed's work. We would request that he add slightly less gore to his art when submitting projects to class but encourage him to pursue his natural artistic expression outside of the classroom."

Morgan's eyes widened as she read the report, and a cold sweat broke out across her forehead. Adam McCormack had been warned about his use of violent imagery and symbolism in his films, just like the killer's videos. It was too much to be a coincidence.

She looked through the rest of the folder, but there was nothing else that suggested a connection to the murders. She was about to give up when she spotted a flash drive tucked into the back flap of the folder.

Morgan's heart raced as she pulled the drive out and made her way over to one of the computers in the corner of the room. She plugged the drive in and waited for the contents to load.

As the files appeared on the screen, Morgan's stomach twisted with anticipation. She clicked on one labeled "The Puppet Master," and the video began to play.

The footage showed a puppet made of string and cloth, moving in jerky motions across a darkened stage. The camera zoomed in on the puppet's face, which was twisted into a grotesque expression of pain and fear. The puppet was being controlled by someone off-camera, and the movements were so lifelike that it was almost as if the puppet was alive.

Morgan clicked the next video, and grainy footage filled the screen. More puppets. This wasn't an exact match to the killer's videos, but these videos were made a long time ago. She thought back to what Gerry had said, something about how David Reed's own style had changed. Morgan knew that people could evolve in their "art," become bolder. She already knew that Adam had suffered some serious trauma when his parents had been murdered in a suspected break-in. The falling out with his mentor after that wouldn't have helped, and she was sure it all contributed to Adam's eventual falling grades, until he dropped out of school altogether.

Now, Adam lived on welfare, mostly off the grid. But the fact that he hadn't been seen, while every cop in the city was now looking for him, made Morgan's stomach curl.

He could be the killer.

The next file she clicked convinced her that he, undoubtably, was.

An image of blood and guts was layered over a strange symbol, much like the ones seen in the killer's video.

Morgan's stomach bottomed out, and she tucked the flash drive into her pocket.

She needed Derik to see this.

***

Morgan slid back into her car, shrouded by the night, and checked her phone.

She had several missed calls from Derik from about thirty minutes ago.

At that time, she'd been busy with Gloria, then hatching her plan to break into the school's records. She tried calling Derik back, but it went straight to voice mail. She left a message, saying, "Greene, call me now. Adam McCormack is the killer; I'm certain of it." She paused, a heavy feeling in her chest "You're the only one I can trust with this."

Morgan sat in her car for what felt like hours, but was really only minutes, waiting for Derik to call back. She kept replaying the footage from the flash drive in her head, her stomach churning with a mixture of fear and excitement. She had finally found something concrete, something that could break the case wide open.

But where was Derik?

As the night wore on, Morgan's anxiety grew. When she couldn't take it anymore, she started her car and headed towards Derik's house. It was a short drive through the city, and traffic was light at this hour. Morgan tried not to think about running through the night from Darren La Roux as she navigated toward Derik's house, then parked out front.

No lights on.

No car in the driveway.

Maybe he was still at HQ, but he would have called. A knot of dread formed in Morgan's stomach.

Where are you, Greene?

Maybe he'd gone to her house when she hadn't picked up. It was only a hunch, but Morgan drove back toward her house, hoping she was right. Because after everything that had happened, there was no way she could hand this information over to Mueller or anyone else at the FBI. It had to be Derik. Maybe she couldn't wholly trust him, but she trusted him more than anyone else in the bureau.

Morgan pulled into her driveway and scanned the street for any sign of Derik's car. Nothing.

She took a deep breath and tried to calm herself down. Maybe he was just busy with something else. Maybe he had left his phone on silent. But as the minutes ticked by and the silence persisted, Morgan's worry turned into full-blown panic.

She couldn't just sit around waiting for him to show up. She had to do something. The flash drive was burning a hole in her pocket, so Morgan made a decision. She would bring the evidence to Derik, even if that meant going straight back to FBI headquarters, where she'd been suspended from earlier.

But before she could pull away, Morgan noticed something on her porch, under the porchlight. A box.

She frowned. She hadn't ordered anything.

With her heart in her throat, Morgan stepped out of her car, into the cool night, and approached the box.

It was a nondescript cardboard box, but when she opened it, Morgan gasped.

Inside, among newspaper clippings and other strange items lay an old film reel. It was dusty and worn with age, and Morgan felt her heart skip a beat as she stared at it, partially expecting it to combust.

But it didn't.

This was a film from the killer--and it had been sent straight to her.

***

Derik's eyes popped open with a gasp.

His vision was blurry, but a large screen materialized in front of him. A movie screen, showing only a white light.

He was in a theater.

Derik's pulse pounded like a jackhammer and every inch of his body was sweaty, but he couldn't move, and he couldn't even close his eyes. He glanced down at his arms, realizing they were bound to a movie seat. His head was pulled back, his eyes forced open, and without being able to see himself, he knew what had happened.

It was the same thing that had happened to all the victims.

The killer, somehow, had caught him.

He kept waiting for the nightmare to end, but it didn't. As the moments ticked on, Derik's adrenaline only rose, and a warmth--almost a euphoria--spread through his veins.

The drug. It was working its way through him.

And like the other victims, it could cause his heart to stop.

Derik's mouth was as dry as sand as he tried to keep the fear under control, because the more he freaked out, the faster his heart would beat, and the faster he would die. He tried to keep his breaths cool, even.

Someone would come for him.

They had to.

"Hello there, Derik Greene," a voice said over an intercom.

Derik flinched. This was it--the voice of the killer.

"W-who are you?" Derik demanded. "What's going on?"

The voice chuckled, sending shivers down Derik's spine. "I'm disappointed in you, Derik. I thought you would have figured it out by now."

"Figured what out?" Derik gritted his teeth, trying to keep his voice steady.

"Who I am, of course." The voice paused for a moment. "But I suppose I can't blame you. You have been chasing your tail, after all."

"What the hell do you want from me?"

The voice chuckled. "You should be asking yourself why you're here, Special Agent Greene. But I suppose that's an easy question to answer, isn't it? You were getting too close to the truth. So, I decided to bring you here, to my theater, where you'll be entertained by my latest film."

Derik's heart sank. He had been right. The killer had been one step ahead of him the whole time. He had no idea how long he had been here, but he knew he had to keep his cool if he was going to survive.

"What do you want from me?" he asked, his voice strained.

"I want to show you my art," the voice said. "You see, I'm not a killer. I'm an artist. A righteous one, at that. And I want you to appreciate my work before you die. Because you do deserve to die, Special Agent Greene. You're not the hero you present yourself as."

Derik's stomach churned. He tried to think of a way out of this, but his mind was foggy from the drugs, yet alert and awake at the same time. But his words got lost in the crosswires, and he couldn't articulate himself properly. He couldn't think of the right words to use to try and manipulate the killer into freeing him. All he could say was:

"You won't get away with this," he said, his voice barely audible.

The voice laughed. "Oh, but I already have, Special Agent Greene. You're just the latest actor in my masterpiece. Let's watch together."

Suddenly, an image appeared on the screen, blinding Derik's eyes. But he had no choice but to look.

It showed a gazelle running across a field.

Cut to a lion with bloody jaws, hunting it.

Then an image of...

Emma?

His ex-wife.

Derik's eyes watered, even though they were propped open and dry. What was this?

Then insects, feasting on a corpse.

Then Morgan, from afar.

Morgan, recently.

Morgan, just the other day.

He recognized her clothes.

"I don't understand," Derik said. "I didn't kill them. They're both alive."

The voice grunted. "Maybe they were, but they were also both guilty. Your wife had an abusive husband, and your partner here is trying to take down the system from within. Just like I am."

"What?" Derik repeated. "What are you talking about?"

"I'm talking about a corrupt system that does nothing but ruin people's lives. I'm talking about a system that'll let a killer like you get away with your crimes time after time after time. I'm talking about a system that will squelch the voices of people who tell the truth."

Derik swallowed. He couldn't believe this was happening, that this was how it ended, and for what? Some deranged art project?

"What are you going to do to me?" he asked, because somehow, his heart was still beating.

"Oh, you know what I'm going to do, Special Agent Greene. I'm going to show you my masterpiece."

A slow cackle filled the room, making Derik's skin crawl.

Then:

"Special Agent Cross is going to join us, and you're both going to die. Together."

CHAPTER TWENTY TWO

Morgan had her spare gun holstered to her belt as she watched the film on an old projector she'd found in her basement, left to her by her dad. The reel clicked as the film played, filling her basement wall with light in the darkness.

None of it made sense.

She had expected to see the strange symbolism, the blood and gore, or videos of someone. Maybe even Darren, somehow. But instead, the film only showed disorganized clips of some other movie, an old horror movie. Morgan recognized some of the actors, but she couldn't place it. She kept watching, waiting for more of a clue, until the film ended, and the room filled with darkness.

"What the hell?" Morgan asked herself, confused and disturbed. She flicked on the lights, then took out her phone and looked up the name of one of the actors she recognized. She scrolled until she saw a familiar image.

It was a cult classic horror movie.

"Theater of Death." Morgan shuddered as she read the synopsis: a group of unsuspecting victims are captured by a deranged artist who forces them to watch his twisted films before killing them in his theater.

It couldn't be a coincidence.

It was an old film, but she remembered that cinema her dad used to take her to downtown would often have late-night viewings of cult classics. On a hunch, she looked up *Theater of Death* movie times in town.

And there, playing right now, was *Theater of Death*. At that same cinema Morgan had once gone to with her father.

Fear gripped her heart. Morgan knew she had to act fast as she darted upstairs, leaving the film behind. She dialed Derik's number, but it went straight to voicemail. She tried again, but still no answer. Skunk barked as Morgan grabbed her keys, then ran out the front door, into the night.

She jumped into her car.

Morgan sped through the empty streets, her mind racing with thoughts of Derik. She had to find him before it was too late. Morgan didn't give a damn if she was suspended. At that moment, she needed her team, so she put her pride aside and called Mueller.

He picked up within a few rings.

"Cross, this better be important--"

"Mueller, the killer has Derik," Morgan said. "I don't need you to ask me how I know, I need you to just trust me."

"Trust you?" Mueller laughed once. "Cross, you are seriously out of line."

"I need you to send a team to the Fairfax Cinema downtown, right now. The killer is there, and he has Derik. Just do it, Mueller."

"I don't take orders from you, Morgan."

"You're taking this one, Mueller. It's for my partner's life. I'll be there in less than ten minutes."

A beat. "I'll send a team. Out of curiosity, what makes you so sure?

"I'll explain everything once this is all over."

Morgan hung up as she swerved into the next lane. She was almost there, but she knew she wouldn't be able to do this alone.

The cinema was nestled downtown, and she pushed her car to its limits as she weaved in and out of traffic. She could only hope that she wasn't too late. She could hear her heart thumping in her chest, and she tried to steady her breathing. She had a feeling she was walking straight into a trap, but she had to find Derik. She had to save him.

The theater had two screens in it, but only one movie was playing, and they were still open. Morgan walked up to the ticket booth, and the bored-looking, teenage attendant looked up at her.

"How many tickets do you need?" he asked.

"I'm not here to watch a movie," Morgan said. She went to grab her badge on instinct, only to realize it wasn't there.

Officially, she wasn't with the FBI right now. But nothing would stop her from getting in.

"Look, I'm with the FBI," Morgan said. "I need you to let me into the theater."

The worker laughed. "And I'm James Bond, but I still gotta pay for tickets. Besides, you're late."

Morgan grunted. She didn't have time for this. She threw money at the kid and didn't even wait for him to print off a ticket--she just stormed inside, finding herself in the lobby, surrounded by the smell of popcorn.

There were two doors. Behind one of them, the sound of the movie. Morgan rushed in, only to see the theater was half-full of civilians. The same strange movie she'd been sent was now playing on the big screen.

Morgan searched the audience, but Derik wasn't among them. She walked up and down the aisle, her eyes scanning each face. Nothing.

The lights were dimmed, and people were engrossed in the movie, though Morgan couldn't focus on it. Every few minutes she'd stop to look around for Derik, but he was nowhere to be seen. Was he even here at all?

Just then, the movie cut to black.

Mutters sounded in the theater.

Morgan looked up with dread as another image filled the screen.

It was Derik. Tied up, his eyes propped open, his face partially beaten in.

She almost thought she'd imagined it. The image went away just as fast, and the movie resumed.

But then, it happened again.

This time, the image was clearer.

Derik was being filmed, his mouth covered with duct tape, his arms and legs tied to a chair with a gag in his mouth. He was trying to scream, but nothing came out. More confused mutters from the crowd.

Confusion cluttered Morgan's mind too. How was he doing this? He must have hacked their screens—but why? He had clearly reached a breaking point of insanity, Morgan thought, and the stakes were too high to brush off.

That really was Derik. She was sure of it.

Then, a black screen with a single message:

There is a bomb in the theater, under one of the seats. The moment that person moves, you all die.

Everyone screamed, and Morgan's heart sank.

"Nobody move!" she shouted over the chaos. Some people scrambled from their seats, and Morgan braced herself, but the explosion didn't come. Those remaining were still, watching Morgan, waiting for their next instruction.

But Morgan had to go.

Derik was in the next room, she was sure of it, but she couldn't just leave these people. Where the hell was her team?

"What do we do?" a woman shouted in despair.

"Please, stay in your seats," Morgan said. "I'm with the FBI. Help is coming. Just please, stay calm!"

But the room kept crying out with despair and chaos. Morgan's head spun. She needed to get control of these people, to ensure no one else stood up.

She took a deep breath and stepped forward. "Listen to me!" she shouted, projecting her voice as loud as she could. The crowd fell silent, their eyes fixed on her. "I need every one of you to stay calm. I know this is scary, but we need to work together to get out of here alive. I'm going to need everyone to exit the theater in an orderly fashion, one row at a time, and leave everything behind. Don't touch anything, don't move anything. We're all going to be okay."

Morgan could feel the panic in the air, but she forced herself to stay calm. She knew that any sudden movements could set off the bomb.

"Good, everyone, you're doing great," Morgan said. "Just stay where you are. Help is on the way."

Morgan's mind raced as she tried to come up with a plan. She couldn't leave the theater and abandon Derik, but she also couldn't risk the lives of all the people in the room. As she scanned the crowd, her eyes met those of a young girl in the front row. The girl couldn't be more than ten, and her eyes were filled with fear.

Morgan needed to save Derik, but she also couldn't leave these people behind. Not until the rest of her team arrived.

She just prayed Mueller had truly answered her call.

Just then, the doors burst open, and several armed agents flooded the theater.

Morgan breathed a sigh of relief as she recognized her team among them. Her heart was thumping in her chest, but she pushed her fear aside. She had to save Derik.

"We need a bomb squad in here now!" Morgan shouted as she ran towards her team. "You need to keep these people calm. I'm going to find Greene."

"Cross, hold on!" one of the team members shouted, but Morgan pushed on, storming through the exit.

Mueller was waiting for her outside. "Where the hell have you been, Morgan?"

"In the theater, and I need to go back in."

"The hell you are," Mueller said, throwing an arm out to stop her. She tried to push it aside, but Mueller was a lot stronger than he looked, and she lost.

"Listen, Cross! I know you think you're some hero, but we don't need more casualties!"

"My partner is in that theater!" Morgan snapped. "He's about to be killed by that psycho. He may have already done it by now. So, excuse me if I don't give a shit about your concerns. I need you to tell your agents to back off and let me do my job."

"Not a chance."

"Listen to me, Mueller! He's gonna kill him if we don't stop him! Now let me go!" Morgan dashed under Mueller's arm and shoved her way into the empty theater. It was dark, with rows upon rows of seats. There was nothing playing on the screen, and no sign of Derik anywhere. Panic hit her as she searched for him, but there was no sign of anyone here at all.

That was when she realized it.

The color of the seats.

They were red here.

But in the shot of Derik on the screen, the seats--they had been green.

Morgan's stomach fell to floor as the realization settled in.

The killer did have Derik. But he wasn't here.

Morgan was sure she'd seen those green seats somewhere before. somewhere recently, but she couldn't put her finger on it. She tried to slow her mind down, to think of all the places she'd been. The theaters she'd looked at with Derik.

There was one... the place she had looked with Derik, before they'd found Owen Fernandez's body at the drive-in theater.

That had to be it.

The abandoned cinema on the outskirts of town.

CHAPTER TWENTY THREE

Morgan blew past Mueller and the rest of the FBI team before they could even think about stopping her.

She didn't care about the repercussions. If Muller wanted to take her badge away permanently, none of it mattered to her, because Derik's life was on the line.

Morgan had her moments of doubt in her partner, but she'd also had moments of trust. And she realized, as she ran to her car in the lot by the theater, that Derik was possibly all she had left, next to her dog.

He was her only friend.

Her dad had died while she was in prison. Mueller had no faith in her, and she didn't know who in the FBI had betrayed her. Morgan had no one--except for him.

She was not about to let him die.

She jumped in her car, the old rattle of the engine making her flinch as she stomped on the accelerator. She wasn't sure how long she'd been in the theater, but she had no idea how long it would take for the bomb squad to diffuse the bomb. And she realized that she wasn't sure how long she had to save Derik. Morgan sped away from the current theater and towards the old abandoned one. She'd gone there once with Derik, and it was the only place she could think of that seemed to fit the description. The only place where she had seen those green seats.

At least, she hoped it was the right place.

She raced through the streets, and, in a short period of time, she was driving down the long, desolate road that led to the old cinema. The long, pothole-ridden road was lined with trees on either side, and the building itself couldn't be seen from the road. Morgan parked at the gate and ran outside, her heart thumping in her chest as the sky cleared, showing the brilliant stars that somehow felt oppressive.

Morgan's heart sank as she reached the building. The only sounds were the chirping of crickets and the rustling of leaves. She hesitated to go in, frozen for a moment, terrified of what she might find.

She could be walking into a scene with Derik's dead body.

Or she could be walking into nothing at all if this was the wrong location.

She didn't know, and she had no time to figure it out.

There was no other way to find out. It was now or never.

Morgan took a deep breath and stepped inside.

The lobby of the cinema was empty and dark. Morgan checked the doors leading in and out, but they were unlocked. She was sure Derik was here.

She strained her ears, trying to hear anything, but she could hear nothing. The place was silent.

Morgan tried to remain calm. There was no sense in panicking.

Her flashlight clicked on, and she shone it around. As her eyes adjusted to the darkness, she could see the old concession stands, the advertising posters on the walls, and the empty ticket booths.

There was no trace of him at all.

She checked the first room. There were green seats, but as Morgan crept down the row, she saw no sign of anyone at all. Morgan's heartbeat thumped in her ears as she shone her flashlight around and realized that she was alone in the theater. *I'm too late,* she thought, her heart sinking.

Derik could be somewhere else. In another building altogether.

He could already be dead.

But those green seats--Morgan was sure they were a match. There were more movie rooms in the abandoned cinema, and she couldn't give up yet. She had to keep looking.

Morgan returned to the lobby and tuned her ears for any sound. She crept her way to the other side of the hall, toward the door at the end.

The door was closed, and Morgan hesitated before she opened it. She had no idea what she would find on the other side.

She took a deep breath and stepped inside.

The room was dark, but Morgan could make out some shapes in the shadows. She moved closer, shining her flashlight around to try to get a better look.

It was just another empty theater. The rows of seats stretched out into a seemingly endless abyss. The once lush, dark green upholstery was now faded and worn, tattered, and ripped in places. It was covered in cobwebs that looked like delicate, gray-white lace, while the dust that lingered in the air gave them an eerie, wavering glow.

He wasn't here, either.

Feeling defeated, Morgan made her way back into the lobby, gun at the ready. There was still one more room to check, but she was losing hope.

Then, she heard it:

A clicking sound.

Like a projector.

Through the crack in the double doors to the theater, Morgan saw light.

Her hope spurred to life.

The killer was here.

He must have seen her arrive.

Maybe he knew she was coming.

There was no way to know.

Maybe he was luring her in, like a spider lures its prey into its web, only to kill it.

But Morgan had no choice.

She had to go in.

She pushed on the double doors, opening them with a slow creak. She shone the light into the theater and then stopped.

There was no one here.

But the projector was on.

As Morgan stepped into the theater, she saw the rows of green seats and the screen, playing one of the killer's signature films. The animals hunting, the symbols.

But then...

A video of her?

Morgan's stomach twisted as she saw herself on the screen. It didn't make sense. Derik hadn't done anything to hurt Morgan, so why would the killer make him view images of her?

Then the image changed to another woman. Someone Morgan only vaguely recognized. It took her a moment to realize it was Derik's ex-wife, Emma, who he said had cheated on him.

Snapping herself out of it, Morgan hurried into the room, only to see him.

Derik was strapped to a seat in the very front row.

"Greene!" Morgan ran up to him with tunnel vision. She skidded right in front of him, terrified of what she'd see.

But Derik was alive.

His eyes, forced open, danced across the screen in front of her, and his mouth was slack.

But he was alive.

"C-Cross," he managed, his eyes finding her.

"Derik, I'm gonna get you out of here!" Morgan shouted.

"I'm... sorry..."

Morgan shook her head. "Don't worry. We're gonna get out of here alive, we're gonna be okay."

She barely finished her sentence before Morgan felt a sharp pain on the back of her head, and everything went black.

CHAPTER TWENTY FOUR

Morgan woke up tied to a chair, her eyes unable to close. Her head felt like it was splitting in two. She was in that same theater, facing the empty screen before her that showed a pale and chilling light. Her head was pounding, and when she tried to touch it, she was restrained by rope.

She was tied up, the same way the others had been.

Morgan's heart pounded in her chest as she wriggled against the rope that was slowly cutting into her wrist. Then:

"Cross..."

Derik's voice.

Morgan couldn't move her head, but she could now sense Derik's presence right beside her. The killer had tied them up, side-by-side, in that same theater, but he was nowhere in sight.

"Derik," Morgan said, trying to stay calm. "Are you hurt?"

"I'm... he... drugged me..."

Morgan's heart fell. If that were the case, then Derik could still die, the same way the others had. Morgan paid attention to her own body, but she didn't feel any drugs coursing through her veins, only these damn restraints holding her in place.

She didn't want to panic, but she had never wanted to be trapped again. Ten years in prison, only for it to end like this?

It wasn't right.

She refused to accept it.

"We're gonna get out of here, Derik," Morgan said.

"No, you aren't." A new voice. Morgan froze.

Slowly, a figure walked in front of the white screen, a momentary silhouette, before Morgan's eyes adjusted, and his face became clear.

Adam McCormack.

He looked older, more haggard than on his file. He was tall and skinny, his face gaunt, his eyes buggy with ratty brown hair and a clean-shaven face that made him look both young and old all at once. He was worn out, like a skeleton. But the way he looked at them scared her.

It was more than amusement. It was almost admiration. Like Morgan and Derik were art pieces for him to appreciate.

"Adam," Morgan said.

He laughed once. "So, you do know who I am."

Morgan gritted her teeth. "You killed those people."

Adam shrugged. "They were just practice, really. I had to get good before going after the real prize."

"The real prize?"

Adam took a step closer. "You, Special Agent Cross. You're the one I've been after all along."

Morgan's heart pounded in her chest. "Why me?"

"Because you're like me. You've seen what it's like to be torn away from society. You know how sick it is, and you want to destroy it from the inside out. Maybe you don't realize it yet, but you do. You want to destroy it, Morgan Cross, because it betrayed you. I know your story."

Morgan wanted to be sick. All this time, she had been looking for Adam McCormack.

Meanwhile, he'd been watching her.

He'd been planning this all along.

"I'm not corrupted," Morgan said. "I'm trying to bring people like you to justice. I'm not trying to destroy anything."

Adam laughed again. "Justice? What does that even mean? You're just a pawn in a game that's rigged against you. You don't even know who's pulling the strings. Don't want to admit it? Now, you're going to pay for what you've done," Adam said, a smile creeping onto his face, as he took out a gun. "You're going to pay for your sins."

Morgan's eyes widened, and she struggled against the ropes that bound her. She had been in dangerous situations before, but this was different. This was personal.

"You're delusional," Morgan spat out. "You don't know me."

"Oh, but I do," Adam said, his voice low. "I know everything about you. Your past, your present, and your future. You're the perfect subject."

"Then what does he have to do with it?" Morgan asked. "Why don't you let Derik go!"

Adam's smile faded. "Derik? Oh, you really don't know, do you? He doesn't mean anything to me, but he's certainly no hero. But you, Morgan, you're special. You're the one I've been waiting for."

Morgan gritted her teeth, struggling against the ropes that bound her. She had to find a way out of this, had to find a way to save Derik and herself.

"You're sick," Morgan said, narrowing her eyes at Adam.

Adam chuckled. "And you're a criminal. The irony is not lost on me, Morgan."

Morgan didn't know what to say to that. She had made mistakes in the past, but she had paid for them. And now she was trying to make a difference, trying to bring criminals like Adam to justice.

"You're not going to get away with this," Morgan said, her voice shaking slightly.

Adam's eyes narrowed. "Oh, but I already have. No one knows where you are, Morgan. No one knows what's happening to you."

Morgan's heart sank. He was right. They were alone, trapped in this theater with no one to help them.

But Morgan wasn't going to give up. She had survived prison, had survived being a target of the killer, and she wasn't going down this easily. She wiggled her hands against the restraints. If she could just get her thumb through, she might be able to loosen them enough to break free and attack him.

She had to keep him talking.

And being hostile wasn't going to work. Psychopaths loved to talk about themselves, and Morgan knew that was just the thing that would buy them some time.

"I know about your parents, Adam," she said, and his eyes flashed to hers. "It's terrible, what happened to them. Shot in front of you when you were only a child, during nothing more than a petty break-in? It's awful, Adam."

Adam's expression softened for a moment, before hardening again. "You think you know me, Morgan? You think you know my pain?"

Morgan kept her voice steady. "No, I don't. But I know what it's like to lose someone you love. And I know it's not worth losing yourself over."

Adam shook his head. "You don't understand anything. You and people like you are the reason why the world is the way it is. You take away everything that's good and beautiful and leave only chaos in your wake. But I can fix that. I can make the world a better place. I can use my art, my movies, to spread beauty and life and meaning."

Morgan didn't believe a word he was saying. All she saw was a man consumed by his own madness. But she had to keep him talking, keep him distracted.

"And how do you plan on doing that?" Morgan asked.

Adam smiled. "By ridding the world of people like you. And then, only the strong will be left. The ones who deserve to live. A world of beautiful art, of beautiful movies."

Morgan's stomach turned. This was a new level of craziness she had never seen before. Adam was so convinced of his own righteousness that he couldn't see how twisted his thinking was.

"And how do I fit into that?" Morgan asked.

Adam took a step closer, the gun still pointed at her. "You're my masterpiece, Morgan. You're the final piece of my puzzle. Once I eliminate you, my art will be complete."

Morgan's mind was racing. She had to think of a way out of this, fast. She didn't know how much time they had left before Adam decided to pull the trigger.

"What if I joined you?" Morgan asked, trying to keep her voice steady. "What if I worked with you on your movies, helped you spread your message?"

Adam tilted his head, considering her offer. "I don't know. You've already proven yourself untrustworthy. And besides, I think you're too entrenched in the old ways of thinking. You couldn't possibly understand my vision. And Special Agent Greene here? He's no hero either. Neither of you are. You just masquerade as such. It's pathetic, truly."

Morgan kept trying to shimmy herself free. She could feel the ropes slacking. Just a bit more...

"You're right," Morgan said, "the world is corrupt. But you're wrong about me. I was wrongfully convicted. I never killed anyone."

Adam's eyes flashed, and he smiled. "You and I both know that's not true."

Morgan's chest seized. He couldn't possibly mean...

Darren?

Had he seen that all happen?

"Don't worry," he said with a wink, "your secret is safe with me."

Slowly, Adam raised the gun--and pointed it right at Derik.

"No!" Morgan yelled, her heart skidding to a stop.

Derik's eyes were wide with fear. Morgan had to do something, had to get Adam's attention back on her--away from Derik.

"Please, Adam," she said, her voice shaking. "Please don't do this."

Adam tilted his head, studying her, as if considering her offer. "Too late for that. You should know that by now."

"No, wait," Morgan said, struggling to get the words out. "I know we've only just met. But maybe that's because we're too similar. Maybe if we joined forces, we could make something truly amazing. Something that everyone would remember."

Adam's smile widened. "That is an interesting idea, Morgan. I will consider it."

Morgan's heart skipped a beat. He was going to buy it. At least for a few more minutes.

But then he said, "But we don't need Special Agent Greene for that, do we?"

Morgan stared at him. He couldn't possibly mean...

"No!" Morgan yelled, her voice cracking.

He pulled the trigger.

Morgan screamed.

CHAPTER TWENTY FIVE

Morgan watched the scene unfold in slow motion. Like her whole life had become nothing more than a twisted film, about to reach its end.

The bullet hit Derik's body. Morgan wasn't sure where--she couldn't move her head, but she could feel everything around her. Derik barely made a sound, but his breathing became sputtered.

A sob escaped Morgan's lips. She struggled to free herself as Adam paced across the white screen, smiling.

"Time to wrap this up," he said, his eyes gleaming.

Morgan fought with all her might. She kicked, she screamed, she scratched at the ropes. She had to get out of here, had to save Derik.

The ropes were almost loose.

Just a bit more.

Adam whipped around, pointing the gun at her again.

"There's my girl," he said, his voice warm with adulation.

Morgan fought against the ropes, against the pain in her shoulders and arms. She had to get away from Adam and save Derik, had to get out of here before it was too late.

Almost there.

She could do it.

"You know, I must say, Morgan, I truly admire you. You were always such a strong woman. That's why I knew you would be my masterpiece."

Adam was too caught up in his own theatrical, delusional monologue to realize that Morgan's right hand was almost free.

"I know how it is," he continued. "It's so difficult to resist the urge to run and save yourself, to feel the adrenaline pumping through you. You're just so human, Morgan. I know it's a struggle to hold it in, but that's what makes you so beautiful. You're part of the world's beauty."

Morgan snapped. She had heard enough.

She jerked her right hand up and--

"No!"

Morgan froze and Adam's smile became wider.

"Did you really think you could get away so easily?" he asked.

Morgan stared at him, wide-eyed. A gun had been pointed at her head before, but this time it felt so much more dire. This time, she knew she wasn't going to get away.

Morgan's muscles burned with effort and the tears in her eyes blurred her vision.

"But why would I want a copy of a masterpiece when I have the original right here?" Adam said, pointing the gun at her.

Morgan's hand was free, but Adam was fully in control. She had to find a way to get the advantage, but anything she did would be a risk of a bullet to the head.

But Morgan had nothing left to lose.

Derik was slumped in the seat beside her, potentially dead.

She'd lost her father.

All she had was Skunk, and she didn't want to leave him behind, but damn it, everything had fallen apart.

She had to risk it.

Morgan ducked down and raised her hand up, just as Adam rang a shot out. Morgan punched his forearm, sending the gun flying.

Hot pain seared past Morgan's ear, and her hearing became dull, ringing. Her head was being cleaved in two. Disoriented, she used her free hand to yank the rope on her other hand, then her legs, then pulled the tape that had been forcing her eyes open.

Fueled by adrenaline, Morgan stood up, only to see Adam cowering away from her.

He'd lost the gun.

When Morgan had punched his forearm, it had flown into the row of seats, and now he was unarmed.

Morgan immediately went after it, reaching for the gun. Adam pulled back at her, so she did what she could--she kicked it so it flew up the row, far out of his reach. She turned back and threw a punch straight at Adam's face, clocking him square in the jaw.

He stumbled back toward the white screen behind him in a daze, and Morgan held her fists up, ready to brawl. Her head hurt and the pain in her ear was defeating, but adrenaline kept her on her feet.

Adam was going to pay for everything he'd done.

Adam had been knocked off balance by Morgan's kick and he managed to right himself. He turned to Morgan and flashed a smile that nearly knocked her off her feet.

"You're such a superb fighter," he said. "I knew I had chosen wisely."

Morgan's blood boiled. "You're going to pay for this," she said, her voice shaking.

"I already have," Adam said. His expression was sad, like a mournful god, but his eyes were still gleaming with evil. "I lost you. And that's something I can't come back from. But I will do anything to have you again."

Something in Adam's tone made Morgan's skin crawl.

Adam rushed her, his hands flying up at her face.

Morgan stepped aside, but Adam had anticipated that--he grabbed her arm, spun her around and locked her in a tight hold.

Morgan struggled against his grip. He was strong, considering how skinny he was, but Morgan hadn't spent ten years in prison lying around doing nothing. She was in the best shape of her life. Using all her strength, she twisted out of Adam's grasp, then shot a knee straight up into his groin.

Taken by surprise, Adam stumbled backward, clutching his stomach.

Morgan stepped back, then shot a kick at his head. Adam ducked, but Morgan was already following through with a flurry of punches. Adam blocked her punches, which only infuriated Morgan. She had to get him on the ground, and she had to do it now.

Morgan darted her arm out and snatched Adam's hand, yanking it toward her and twisting it behind his back. She pulled back hard--she heard Adam's shoulder pop.

Morgan wasn't going to let her opening get away. She reared back and kicked him full in the chest, launching him back and into the white screen.

Adam's body crashed into the screen and a low, echoing crack sent shivers down Morgan's spine.

Adam didn't move.

"You're going to pay for this," Morgan said between gasps for air.

At least, that's what she tried to say. It came out more as a croak. She couldn't hear much, with her ears ringing, but her heart pounded hard against her ear. It sounded like a drum.

Morgan kicked Adam's body into the white screen again, and this time it gave in and crumbled beneath his weight.

The gun wasn't far away.

Morgan stumbled over to it, her ears still ringing.

She grabbed the gun and worked the safety, flicked it off.

There was nothing else in the black room.

Nothing but Derik, slumped forward in the seat, unmoving.

She couldn't hear anything, but she could tell he was breathing.

Adam had done a number on her, but it was nothing compared to what he'd done to Derik. To those other people.

Morgan pointed the gun down at Adam as he lifted himself on all fours, coughing up blood.

She wanted to shoot.

More than anything, she wanted to put him down right here. He deserved it, for what he'd done. And if Derik was really dead, then she'd always want Adam's blood.

But then she saw a flash of Darren in her mind.

Of cold cell walls.

No...

She couldn't do it. Not again.

She had to do this the right way.

Morgan grabbed some of the rope Adam had used to tie her and began restraining him.

She tied up his wrists together, then his legs, then his hands to his legs, so he couldn't move.

It was only when she was done that she realized he'd been smiling the whole time.

"You're making a grave mistake," he said, once he'd caught his breath.

"Shut the hell up," Morgan spat. "Just shut the hell up. You're lucky I'm not putting a bullet in your head."

Adam only laughed. "You want to, don't you? Because you're a monster, Morgan Cross. I could smell it off you the moment I saw you." His eyes widened. "That's it, isn't it? That's why you're so afraid of what you are."

Morgan placed her hands to her temples.

Was he right?

No. She wasn't a monster. She had just done the right thing.

She couldn't kill him.

But he deserved it.

She couldn't do it.

She stepped back, her heart pounding in her chest. She tried not to think, to let her instincts take over. Her heart was pumping blood through her body with every beat. He was right--she did want to kill him.

But she wouldn't.

There was still Derik.

Morgan turned away from Adam to Derik's limp body. She rushed over to him, forgetting the psychopath she'd just tied up, and tore a piece of fabric from her shirt so she could tourniquet his wound. Once it was sealed off, she checked his pulse.

If there was one, she couldn't feel it.

All she could do was hold him, repeating in her mind over and over again that this was all her fault.

<h1 style="text-align:center">CHAPTER TWENTY SIX</h1>

Morgan stood outside of the hospital room, her head hanging low in shame. Through the windows, the darkness of night still shrouded the sky, even though it had been hours since she'd escaped from that abandoned cinema.

There was a bandage wrapped around Morgan's head. In her fight with Adam, he'd shot her, and the bullet had grazed her ear. She was going to live, but it hurt like hell, especially after the adrenaline wore off and she was left with the memories of what she'd done.

Of what she couldn't do.

She could hear the beeping from beyond the room, and she wanted nothing more than to storm in there, but she couldn't, not yet. Derik was in critical condition. The nurses and doctors were doing everything they could to save him, and all Morgan could do was stand here and wait.

The doctors were talking about the "worst case scenario," which meant Derik would be in a coma for weeks and would never remember who he was or where he'd come from.

Morgan refused to believe that. She refused to believe he'd just… disappear from her life.

Not like this.

Her hands were shaking. She felt sick. She felt empty.

She knew the doctors were right. It might be possible that Derik wouldn't remember her, but she would never forget him. Apparently, there had been extremely high levels of amphetamine in his veins, and Adam's gunshot had pierced Derik's lung. He'd lost a lot of blood.

But there was hope.

The "best case" was a recovery. Since Derik was healthy, there was hope he would be okay.

Morgan had to hold onto that.

With Adam apprehended, at least she could feel safe, for real. His motivations in the end seemed to be lost, even on him; he'd started off targeting people who he viewed as corrupt, but he'd gotten so drunk on power, that he'd turned it to innocents. The bomb threat had been real—the team had dismantled it, and it turned out to have been placed underneath a man's seat in the theater. Thankfully, that man had listened to Morgan's instructions to stay calm and cooperated with the rest of the team when they'd arrived. Because of that, no more people had to die by him.

Thank God for that.

"Cross," a voice said.

Morgan looked up to see AD Mueller, his expression stern as his broad frame walked down the hallway toward her. Morgan's jaw tightened. She didn't want to deal with his shit right now.

"Mueller," Morgan muttered, turning away.

"I see your ear is okay," Mueller said. "I guess I don't need to remind you how much trouble you're in, operating like you were an FBI agent after I suspended you."

"Derik would be dead if I hadn't found him," Morgan shot back. Inside, she still blamed herself, but she blamed the FBI too. They hadn't been looking for Derik. Morgan had been.

"True," Mueller said, "but you still broke protocol. You assaulted a man when you didn't even have a badge."

"I assaulted a monster," Morgan said, "and it was self-defense. He'd tied me and Greene up. He was a monster, Mueller. I won't take shit for this. I just won't."

Mueller shook his head slowly. "I'm not here to judge you, Cross. But you are walking a thin line. You know that. Right now, you're lucky I'm not charging you with trespassing, assault, and obstruction of justice."

"Derik is alive, Mueller. He's in there--"

"Because you dragged him out of there," Mueller said. He lifted an eyebrow. "You both could have been killed."

"But I wasn't," Morgan said. "And neither was Derik. You should have gotten there faster."

Mueller took a deep breath and loosened his tie. "Look, you've gotten yourself into a lot of trouble, but right now, the last thing I want is for you to be in more. You're a good agent, Morgan, but you're out of line. Reckless. You can't follow rules. There's no place for that in the FBI."

"Then maybe I'm just not cut out for it, sir," Morgan fired back, turning away. She didn't care anymore.

She'd dedicated so much of herself to the FBI before she'd gone to prison.

Then, they'd thrown her away. Would barely even listen to her pleas of innocence. Stole ten years of her life from her, and for what?

Morgan hated to admit it, but Adam was right about one thing. Why would she stay loyal to a system that had no loyalty for her? If she was disposable to them, then she didn't care anymore.

All she wanted was to know if Derik would be okay, not be chastised for saving his life and her own.

Mueller sighed. "I don't know what to do with you, Cross."

"Then do nothing," Morgan said. "Leave me alone."

"This is my job, Special Agent Cross," Mueller said. "You need to understand that. You need to understand that what I do is for the greater good. Do you really want to be a vigilante?"

"And do you really want to ignore the case?"

"That's not what I'm doing," Mueller said. "I'm just saying you can't act unilaterally, Cross. You can't go against the FBI like that. You're lucky we're not going to treat you like a criminal and detain you for your own protection."

"Why don't you?" Morgan said.

Mueller looked at her, long and hard, before he turned away. "I'll follow up with you later. Just... stay out of trouble."

Finally, he walked away, leaving Morgan seeing red. She hated Mueller, and she hated the FBI. Maybe there was no place for her there after all.

***

"Morgan Cross?"

Morgan lifted her head at the sound of her voice, gathering her bearings. She must have dozed off in the waiting room. A young nurse stood before her, holding her hands together, a slight smile on her face that gave Morgan hope.

"Is Derik okay?" Morgan asked.

She tried to stand quickly, but the pain in her head almost made her black out. The nurse caught her. She helped Morgan steady herself before she walked her toward the hospital room.

"He's stable, for now," the nurse said. "He hasn't woken up yet, but we have hope he will."

Morgan nodded. She followed the nurse into the room, her heart pounding. Her hands were shaking. She didn't want to get her hopes up, but the nurse's words were like music to her ears.

The other nurse was by Derik's side, taking his pulse. Morgan swallowed hard as she saw his face, and the massive bandages around his chest. He was unconscious, but still breathing.

"You're the only one here to see him," the nurse said to Morgan. "I'm sure he'll be happy to see a friendly face when he wakes up."

The other nurse smiled at Morgan. Morgan nodded. "I'll keep it as quiet as I can."

"Good," the nurse said. She gave Morgan a pat on the back, heading toward the door. "He's been through a lot. We're just glad to see him alive."

Morgan stood over Derik's bed, watching his chest rise and fall with his breaths. She couldn't believe he was alive. The thought that the last time she'd seen him, when he'd been nearly dead, was one she didn't want to think about. Not yet.

She sat down in a chair next to the bed and took Derik's hand. They'd been through so much together. Before Morgan went to prison, they'd been partners for years, and now that she was out, he was there on the other side, waiting.

She couldn't lose him.

It didn't matter what Gloria had said. Or whatever bullshit Adam had ranted about.

Morgan just wanted to see Derik okay.

Morgan wasn't going to give up on him.

Derik's eyes flickered open, and Morgan's heart leapt in her chest. She squeezed his hand tightly.

"Derik?" she said. "Derik, can you hear me?"

Derik's eyes settled on her. He blinked, but he didn't say anything. His eyes looked glazed over.

Derik's face was pale, his mouth dry and cracked.

Morgan squeezed his hand tighter. "I'm here, Derik. It's me. Morgan."

Derik swallowed. His Adam's apple bobbed as he worked to form a word.

"Hey, Cross," he said.

"Yeah," Morgan said, her voice breaking as she lifted his hand to her face. She kissed his knuckles. "I'm here."

Derik's eyes moved over Morgan's face. He moved his lips, but no sound came out.

"You're gonna be okay, D," Morgan said. "Adam was arrested. We got him."

Derik smiled, melting back into the bed. "Damn it, Cross. I told you not to do anything stupid and reckless. Look at your head."

Morgan was confused for a moment before she remembered the bandages. She laughed. "He grazed my ear with a bullet, no big deal."

Derik nodded. "Thank God for that," he said. "If Adam had killed you, I'd be in a world of trouble. You know that, right?"

Morgan gave a weak smile. Derik's heart was already moving faster. She squeezed his hand.

"I'm here now, Derik. And I'm not going anywhere."

Derik's eyes searched hers for a moment before his gaze moved to their clasped hands. "Morgan," he said, his voice barely above a whisper. "I'm sorry."

Morgan frowned. "Sorry for what?"

Derik took a deep breath. "I'm sorry for not believing you. For not trusting you."

Morgan's heart skipped a beat. "You don't have to apologize for that, Derik. Mueller's furious with me for working off the books, but I had to do it. I should've told you what I planned on doing. We'd agreed on no secrets, but I guess... I guess I didn't trust you." Morgan held her head low in shame.

Derik closed his eyes, his breathing shallow, but steady. Morgan watched over him, waiting for him to speak again.

"Thank you," he said, his voice barely above a whisper. "For saving me. For coming back."

"I'd never let you get away from me that easily."

Derik's eyes fluttered open again. "I missed you," he said. "When you were in prison, I missed you so much."

Morgan's heart swelled with emotion. She wanted to tell him everything, about how much she'd missed him too, about the nightmares and the loneliness.

"I missed you too, D," she said instead. "But we're together now. That's all that matters."

Derik nodded, his eyes closing again, like he was at peace.

For a moment, Morgan was too.

EPILOGUE

Morgan slid the key into the door of Derik's house, then pushed it opened, welcomed by the masculine scent of his home. His stay at the hospital had been extended, and he'd given Morgan a key to his place, asking her to go get some clean clothes and books for him to read. She'd obliged without question. It was the least she could do.

It had been a few days since Adam had been apprehended, and Morgan felt at ease as she walked through Derik's home, morning light seeping through the windows. It really was a bachelor pad, and he hadn't done much to clean up before he'd ended up in the hospital.

Clothes were strewn across the floor, and dishes were piled high in the sink. Morgan couldn't help but smile at the mess. She'd have to clean it up later, but for now, she was just happy that Derik was going to be okay.

Morgan made her way to the bedroom, opening the closet door. She picked out a few of Derik's shirts and a pair of jeans, then turned to the bedside table. A few books were stacked on top, and Morgan couldn't resist picking one up. It was a detective novel, one that she'd read before. She flipped it open, scanning the pages, finding it vaguely amusing that Derik would read something like this. Shaking her head, she tucked the book away into her bag and kept looking for other things he might need during his hospital stay.

She smiled as she saw his favorite hoodie hanging in the closet, along with some of his other clothes. She grabbed them and folded them neatly, placing them into her bag before moving away from the closet.

Morgan glanced around the room, taking in all of Derik's belongings and trying to pick out anything else that he might need. Focusing on the desk in the corner, she searched through it and found a few more books that Derik had been reading recently. She quickly tucked these away into her bag as well before heading over to the dresser against one wall. She opened a few drawers and scooped out some warm socks and a pair of slippers. She looked around the room for other items, her gaze landing on the dresser.

When she opened the bottom drawer, she stopped.

Inside, underneath some clothes, was a file folder. An odd place to keep one of those.

Morgan glanced around the room, as if to make sure she was truly alone. She should just put it away--it wasn't her business. But something gnawed at her and beckoned her to take a peek. Morgan knew she had her own share of secrets, and that Derik probably had his too. It was unfair of her to spy on him, but at the same time, she needed to confirm it. Even if it was wrong.

She picked up the folder and opened it, her eyes widening when she saw what was inside.

It was a person's file, equipped with a mugshot and everything.

Morgan's stomach bottomed out at the face that looked back at her, mean-mugging at the camera, uncaring.

This wasn't just any file.

This was Darren La Roux's file.

The man who'd tried to kill her.

NOW AVAILABLE!

FOR WRATH
(A Morgan Cross FBI Suspense Thriller—Book Four)

A serial killer obsessed with immortality. Victims being targeted by a mysterious M.O. An ex-con FBI agent determined to break all the rules….

"A masterpiece of thriller and mystery."
—Books and Movie Reviews, Roberto Mattos (re Once Gone)

FOR WRATH is book #4 in a long-anticipated new series by #1 bestseller and USA Today bestselling author Blake Pierce, whose bestseller Once Gone (a free download) has received over 7,000 five star ratings and reviews.

Superstar FBI Agent Morgan Cross was at the height of her career when she was framed, wrongly imprisoned, and sent to do 10 hard years in prison. Finally exonerated and set free, Morgan emerges from jail as a changed person—hardened, ruthless, closed off to the world, and unsure how to start again. When the FBI comes knocking, desperately needing Morgan to return and hunt down a killer who seems to be obsessed with aging, Morgan is torn.

Morgan is not the same person, no longer willing to play by the rules, and will stop at nothing this time. In a non-stop thriller, it will be a deadly cat and mouse chase between a diabolical killer and an ex-con FBI agent who has nothing left to lose—with a new victim's fate riding on it all.

A page-turning and harrowing crime thriller featuring a brilliant and tortured FBI agent, the Morgan Cross series is a riveting mystery, packed with non-stop action, suspense, twists and turns, revelations, and driven by a breakneck pace that will keep you flipping pages late into the night. Fans of Rachel Caine, Teresa Driscoll and Robert Dugoni are sure to fall in love.

Future books in the series are also available!

"An edge of your seat thriller in a new series that keeps you turning pages! ...So many twists, turns and red herrings... I can't wait to see what happens next."
—Reader review (Her Last Wish)

"A strong, complex story about two FBI agents trying to stop a serial killer. If you want an author to capture your attention and have you guessing, yet trying to put the pieces together, Pierce is your author!"
—Reader review (Her Last Wish)

"A typical Blake Pierce twisting, turning, roller coaster ride suspense thriller. Will have you turning the pages to the last sentence of the last chapter!!!"
—Reader review (City of Prey)

"Right from the start we have an unusual protagonist that I haven't seen done in this genre before. The action is nonstop... A very atmospheric novel that will keep you turning pages well into the wee hours."
—Reader review (City of Prey)

"Everything that I look for in a book... a great plot, interesting characters, and grabs your interest right away. The book moves along at a breakneck pace and stays that way until the end. Now on go I to book two!"
—Reader review (Girl, Alone)

"Exciting, heart pounding, edge of your seat book... a must read for mystery and suspense readers!"
—Reader review (Girl, Alone)

Blake Pierce

Blake Pierce is the USA Today bestselling author of the RILEY PAGE mystery series, which includes seventeen books. Blake Pierce is also the author of the MACKENZIE WHITE mystery series, comprising fourteen books; of the AVERY BLACK mystery series, comprising six books; of the KERI LOCKE mystery series, comprising five books; of the MAKING OF RILEY PAIGE mystery series, comprising six books; of the KATE WISE mystery series, comprising seven books; of the CHLOE FINE psychological suspense mystery, comprising six books; of the JESSIE HUNT psychological suspense thriller series, comprising twenty-eight books; of the AU PAIR psychological suspense thriller series, comprising three books; of the ZOE PRIME mystery series, comprising six books; of the ADELE SHARP mystery series, comprising sixteen books, of the EUROPEAN VOYAGE cozy mystery series, comprising six books; of the LAURA FROST FBI suspense thriller, comprising eleven books; of the ELLA DARK FBI suspense thriller, comprising sixteen books (and counting); of the A YEAR IN EUROPE cozy mystery series, comprising nine books, of the AVA GOLD mystery series, comprising six books; of the RACHEL GIFT mystery series, comprising ten books (and counting); of the VALERIE LAW mystery series, comprising nine books (and counting); of the PAIGE KING mystery series, comprising eight books (and counting); of the MAY MOORE mystery series, comprising eleven books; of the CORA SHIELDS mystery series, comprising eight books (and counting); of the NICKY LYONS mystery series, comprising eight books (and counting), of the CAMI LARK mystery series, comprising eight books (and counting), of the AMBER YOUNG mystery series, comprising five books (and counting), of the DAISY FORTUNE mystery series, comprising five books (and counting), of the FIONA RED mystery series, comprising eight books (and counting), of the FAITH BOLD mystery series, comprising eight books (and counting), of the JULIETTE HART mystery series, comprising five books (and counting), of the MORGAN CROSS mystery series, comprising five books (and counting), and of the new FINN WRIGHT mystery series, comprising five books (and counting).

An avid reader and lifelong fan of the mystery and thriller genres, Blake loves to hear from you, so please feel free to visit

BOOKS BY BLAKE PIERCE

FINN WRIGHT MYSTERY SERIES
WHEN YOU'RE MINE (Book #1)
WHEN YOU'RE SAFE (Book #2)
WHEN YOU'RE CLOSE (Book #3)
WHEN YOU'RE SLEEPING (Book #4)
WHEN YOU'RE SANE (Book #5)

MORGAN CROSS MYSTERY SERIES
FOR YOU (Book #1)
FOR RAGE (Book #2)
FOR LUST (Book #3)
FOR WRATH (Book #4)
FOREVER (Book #5)

JULIETTE HART MYSTERY SERIES
NOTHING TO FEAR (Book #1)
NOTHING THERE (Book #2)
NOTHING WATCHING (Book #3)
NOTHING HIDING (Book #4)
NOTHING LEFT (Book #5)

FAITH BOLD MYSTERY SERIES
SO LONG (Book #1)
SO COLD (Book #2)
SO SCARED (Book #3)
SO NORMAL (Book #4)
SO FAR GONE (Book #5)
SO LOST (Book #6)
SO ALONE (Book #7)
SO FORGOTTEN (Book #8)

FIONA RED MYSTERY SERIES
LET HER GO (Book #1)
LET HER BE (Book #2)

LET HER HOPE (Book #3)
LET HER WISH (Book #4)
LET HER LIVE (Book #5)
LET HER RUN (Book #6)
LET HER HIDE (Book #7)
LET HER BELIEVE (Book #8)

DAISY FORTUNE MYSTERY SERIES
NEED YOU (Book #1)
CLAIM YOU (Book #2)
CRAVE YOU (Book #3)
CHOOSE YOU (Book #4)
CHASE YOU (Book #5)

AMBER YOUNG MYSTERY SERIES
ABSENT PITY (Book #1)
ABSENT REMORSE (Book #2)
ABSENT FEELING (Book #3)
ABSENT MERCY (Book #4)
ABSENT REASON (Book #5)

CAMI LARK MYSTERY SERIES
JUST ME (Book #1)
JUST OUTSIDE (Book #2)
JUST RIGHT (Book #3)
JUST FORGET (Book #4)
JUST ONCE (Book #5)
JUST HIDE (Book #6)
JUST NOW (Book #7)
JUST HOPE (Book #8)

NICKY LYONS MYSTERY SERIES
ALL MINE (Book #1)
ALL HIS (Book #2)
ALL HE SEES (Book #3)
ALL ALONE (Book #4)
ALL FOR ONE (Book #5)
ALL HE TAKES (Book #6)
ALL FOR ME (Book #7)
ALL IN (Book #8)

CORA SHIELDS MYSTERY SERIES
UNDONE (Book #1)
UNWANTED (Book #2)
UNHINGED (Book #3)
UNSAID (Book #4)
UNGLUED (Book #5)
UNSTABLE (Book #6)
UNKNOWN (Book #7)
UNAWARE (Book #8)

MAY MOORE SUSPENSE THRILLER
NEVER RUN (Book #1)
NEVER TELL (Book #2)
NEVER LIVE (Book #3)
NEVER HIDE (Book #4)
NEVER FORGIVE (Book #5)
NEVER AGAIN (Book #6)
NEVER LOOK BACK (Book #7)
NEVER FORGET (Book #8)
NEVER LET GO (Book #9)
NEVER PRETEND (Book #10)
NEVER HESITATE (Book #11)

PAIGE KING MYSTERY SERIES
THE GIRL HE PINED (Book #1)
THE GIRL HE CHOSE (Book #2)
THE GIRL HE TOOK (Book #3)
THE GIRL HE WISHED (Book #4)
THE GIRL HE CROWNED (Book #5)
THE GIRL HE WATCHED (Book #6)
THE GIRL HE WANTED (Book #7)
THE GIRL HE CLAIMED (Book #8)

VALERIE LAW MYSTERY SERIES
NO MERCY (Book #1)
NO PITY (Book #2)
NO FEAR (Book #3)
NO SLEEP (Book #4)
NO QUARTER (Book #5)

NO CHANCE (Book #6)
NO REFUGE (Book #7)
NO GRACE (Book #8)
NO ESCAPE (Book #9)

RACHEL GIFT MYSTERY SERIES
HER LAST WISH (Book #1)
HER LAST CHANCE (Book #2)
HER LAST HOPE (Book #3)
HER LAST FEAR (Book #4)
HER LAST CHOICE (Book #5)
HER LAST BREATH (Book #6)
HER LAST MISTAKE (Book #7)
HER LAST DESIRE (Book #8)
HER LAST REGRET (Book #9)
HER LAST HOUR (Book #10)

AVA GOLD MYSTERY SERIES
CITY OF PREY (Book #1)
CITY OF FEAR (Book #2)
CITY OF BONES (Book #3)
CITY OF GHOSTS (Book #4)
CITY OF DEATH (Book #5)
CITY OF VICE (Book #6)

A YEAR IN EUROPE
A MURDER IN PARIS (Book #1)
DEATH IN FLORENCE (Book #2)
VENGEANCE IN VIENNA (Book #3)
A FATALITY IN SPAIN (Book #4)

ELLA DARK FBI SUSPENSE THRILLER
GIRL, ALONE (Book #1)
GIRL, TAKEN (Book #2)
GIRL, HUNTED (Book #3)
GIRL, SILENCED (Book #4)
GIRL, VANISHED (Book 5)
GIRL ERASED (Book #6)
GIRL, FORSAKEN (Book #7)
GIRL, TRAPPED (Book #8)

GIRL, EXPENDABLE (Book #9)
GIRL, ESCAPED (Book #10)
GIRL, HIS (Book #11)
GIRL, LURED (Book #12)
GIRL, MISSING (Book #13)
GIRL, UNKNOWN (Book #14)
GIRL, DECEIVED (Book #15)
GIRL, FORLORN (Book #16)

LAURA FROST FBI SUSPENSE THRILLER
ALREADY GONE (Book #1)
ALREADY SEEN (Book #2)
ALREADY TRAPPED (Book #3)
ALREADY MISSING (Book #4)
ALREADY DEAD (Book #5)
ALREADY TAKEN (Book #6)
ALREADY CHOSEN (Book #7)
ALREADY LOST (Book #8)
ALREADY HIS (Book #9)
ALREADY LURED (Book #10)
ALREADY COLD (Book #11)

EUROPEAN VOYAGE COZY MYSTERY SERIES
MURDER (AND BAKLAVA) (Book #1)
DEATH (AND APPLE STRUDEL) (Book #2)
CRIME (AND LAGER) (Book #3)
MISFORTUNE (AND GOUDA) (Book #4)
CALAMITY (AND A DANISH) (Book #5)
MAYHEM (AND HERRING) (Book #6)

ADELE SHARP MYSTERY SERIES
LEFT TO DIE (Book #1)
LEFT TO RUN (Book #2)
LEFT TO HIDE (Book #3)
LEFT TO KILL (Book #4)
LEFT TO MURDER (Book #5)
LEFT TO ENVY (Book #6)
LEFT TO LAPSE (Book #7)
LEFT TO VANISH (Book #8)
LEFT TO HUNT (Book #9)

LEFT TO FEAR (Book #10)
LEFT TO PREY (Book #11)
LEFT TO LURE (Book #12)
LEFT TO CRAVE (Book #13)
LEFT TO LOATHE (Book #14)
LEFT TO HARM (Book #15)
LEFT TO RUIN (Book #16)

THE AU PAIR SERIES
ALMOST GONE (Book#1)
ALMOST LOST (Book #2)
ALMOST DEAD (Book #3)

ZOE PRIME MYSTERY SERIES
FACE OF DEATH (Book#1)
FACE OF MURDER (Book #2)
FACE OF FEAR (Book #3)
FACE OF MADNESS (Book #4)
FACE OF FURY (Book #5)
FACE OF DARKNESS (Book #6)

A JESSIE HUNT PSYCHOLOGICAL SUSPENSE SERIES
THE PERFECT WIFE (Book #1)
THE PERFECT BLOCK (Book #2)
THE PERFECT HOUSE (Book #3)
THE PERFECT SMILE (Book #4)
THE PERFECT LIE (Book #5)
THE PERFECT LOOK (Book #6)
THE PERFECT AFFAIR (Book #7)
THE PERFECT ALIBI (Book #8)
THE PERFECT NEIGHBOR (Book #9)
THE PERFECT DISGUISE (Book #10)
THE PERFECT SECRET (Book #11)
THE PERFECT FAÇADE (Book #12)
THE PERFECT IMPRESSION (Book #13)
THE PERFECT DECEIT (Book #14)
THE PERFECT MISTRESS (Book #15)
THE PERFECT IMAGE (Book #16)
THE PERFECT VEIL (Book #17)
THE PERFECT INDISCRETION (Book #18)

THE PERFECT RUMOR (Book #19)
THE PERFECT COUPLE (Book #20)
THE PERFECT MURDER (Book #21)
THE PERFECT HUSBAND (Book #22)
THE PERFECT SCANDAL (Book #23)
THE PERFECT MASK (Book #24)
THE PERFECT RUSE (Book #25)
THE PERFECT VENEER (Book #26)
THE PERFECT PEOPLE (Book #27)
THE PERFECT WITNESS (Book #28)

CHLOE FINE PSYCHOLOGICAL SUSPENSE SERIES
NEXT DOOR (Book #1)
A NEIGHBOR'S LIE (Book #2)
CUL DE SAC (Book #3)
SILENT NEIGHBOR (Book #4)
HOMECOMING (Book #5)
TINTED WINDOWS (Book #6)

KATE WISE MYSTERY SERIES
IF SHE KNEW (Book #1)
IF SHE SAW (Book #2)
IF SHE RAN (Book #3)
IF SHE HID (Book #4)
IF SHE FLED (Book #5)
IF SHE FEARED (Book #6)
IF SHE HEARD (Book #7)

THE MAKING OF RILEY PAIGE SERIES
WATCHING (Book #1)
WAITING (Book #2)
LURING (Book #3)
TAKING (Book #4)
STALKING (Book #5)
KILLING (Book #6)

RILEY PAIGE MYSTERY SERIES
ONCE GONE (Book #1)
ONCE TAKEN (Book #2)
ONCE CRAVED (Book #3)

ONCE LURED (Book #4)
ONCE HUNTED (Book #5)
ONCE PINED (Book #6)
ONCE FORSAKEN (Book #7)
ONCE COLD (Book #8)
ONCE STALKED (Book #9)
ONCE LOST (Book #10)
ONCE BURIED (Book #11)
ONCE BOUND (Book #12)
ONCE TRAPPED (Book #13)
ONCE DORMANT (Book #14)
ONCE SHUNNED (Book #15)
ONCE MISSED (Book #16)
ONCE CHOSEN (Book #17)

MACKENZIE WHITE MYSTERY SERIES
BEFORE HE KILLS (Book #1)
BEFORE HE SEES (Book #2)
BEFORE HE COVETS (Book #3)
BEFORE HE TAKES (Book #4)
BEFORE HE NEEDS (Book #5)
BEFORE HE FEELS (Book #6)
BEFORE HE SINS (Book #7)
BEFORE HE HUNTS (Book #8)
BEFORE HE PREYS (Book #9)
BEFORE HE LONGS (Book #10)
BEFORE HE LAPSES (Book #11)
BEFORE HE ENVIES (Book #12)
BEFORE HE STALKS (Book #13)
BEFORE HE HARMS (Book #14)

AVERY BLACK MYSTERY SERIES
CAUSE TO KILL (Book #1)
CAUSE TO RUN (Book #2)
CAUSE TO HIDE (Book #3)
CAUSE TO FEAR (Book #4)
CAUSE TO SAVE (Book #5)
CAUSE TO DREAD (Book #6)

KERI LOCKE MYSTERY SERIES

A TRACE OF DEATH (Book #1)
A TRACE OF MURDER (Book #2)
A TRACE OF VICE (Book #3)
A TRACE OF CRIME (Book #4)
A TRACE OF HOPE (Book #5)

Made in the USA
Monee, IL
06 October 2023

44071443R00102